The King took several quick steps toward Anna.

"I do not know I have promised. I do not know former condition. I do not know anything but you are my servant"—the voice was climbing higher—"and it is our pleasure that you must live in this Palace, *and you shall obey!*" The last three words were shouted at her.

She backed off a little, trembling. "If I give up now," she thought, "I'm lost." She gathered what was left of her courage and managed to say in a voice so calm that it surprised her, "Your Majesty has perhaps forgotten that I am not a servant, but a governess. I expect to obey Your Majesty's commands within the obligation of my duty to your family, but beyond that I can promise no obedience."

Anna and the King

MARGARET LANDON

Anna and the King

illustrated by
MARGARET AYER

adapted by
STEPHANIE SPINNER

HarperTrophy®
A Division of HarperCollinsPublishers

CONTENTS

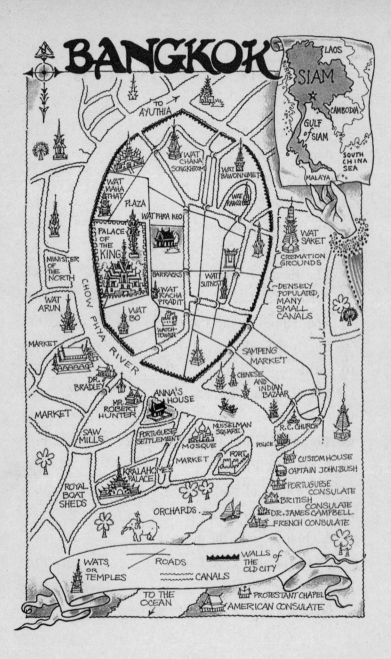

FOREWORD

The story you are about to read is more than just a tale—it comes straight from the pages of history. From 1862 to 1867, Anna Leonowens worked at the Siamese palace, where she was hired by King Mongkut of Siam to teach his children English. It was a very different world from what she had known. The king had absolute power. Slavery was commonplace. But Anna brought her own ideals with her, and the very fact that King Mongkut hired her was a sign that the country would move in a new direction during the next few decades.

Today Siam is known as Thailand, a bustling country in the heart of Southeast Asia. The citizens of Thailand are free and live under a constitutional monarchy, a form of government that is based upon the system in Great Britain. But this was not always so. The changes which King Mongkut made during his reign helped set the stage for a country in which slavery would become a thing of the past and education a priority of the future.

The first settlers of Siam arrived in the country from Central China around two thousand years ago and began to build cities and develop their own culture. Soon people from neighboring regions, including Burma and Cambodia, arrived, and for years several expanding empires clashed. Eventually, the kingdom of Siam was created, and in the

late eighteenth century, the Chakri Dynasty was established. Descendants of the first Chakri king have reigned
ever since.

King Mongkut, the fourth king in this dynasty, ruled
from 1851 to 1868. For twenty-seven years before he was
crowned, King Mongkut was a Buddhist monk, and during
that time he learned both Eastern and Western languages
and studied Western sciences. Though Siam was still an
independent nation when he took the throne, the French,
English, and Dutch had begun to colonize many of the sur-
rounding countries. So King Mongkut decided to cultivate
diplomatic relationships with countries like Great Britain
and the United States. The letters he sends to Abraham
Lincoln and Queen Victoria in this book are examples of
the friendly ties he established so that he could count on
support from these rulers if another country tried to colonize Siam.

In addition to trying to protect Siam's independence,
King Mongkut made other advancements in his country.
He set up printing presses, helped expand trade with
Western countries, organized a police force, and built roads
and canals. By encouraging Christian missionaries in their
educational and medical work among this Buddhist people,
the king reaffirmed his policy of religious freedom.

King Mongkut's son, Prince Chulalongkorn, was
taught English by Anna Leonowens. When he took the
throne years later, one of his first major acts was to declare

that slavery would be abolished in Siam. And, recognizing the importance of his own education, he began the process of educating his people by opening schools. In 1932, under a later king, the system of government was changed to a constitutional monarchy and the people finally shared in the decision making. In 1939, Siam became Thailand, which means "land of the free."

In 1870, Anna Leonowens published *The English Governess at the Siamese Court*, the first of two books about her experiences in Siam. Many years later Margaret Landon discovered these books while living in Siam and became intrigued with Anna's life. She decided to combine the two books into one volume and update the language to make Anna's adventures more accessible to modern readers. In 1943, *Anna and the King of Siam* was published. Later, a version for younger readers was issued. The book became a best-seller, and the basis for a Broadway musical and famous movie, *The King and I*.

As you read this story from long ago, it may seem hard to see the king as a modern thinker. But think about what it must have been like before there were printing presses or roads or schools. Then imagine how one small act, like bringing in a foreign teacher to educate a family, may have changed the course of Siam's history. Without this exposure to new ways of thinking, would Prince Chulalongkorn have so readily freed his people or established schools? Perhaps. Or perhaps not . . .

ONE

BANGKOK, SIAM

It was March 15, 1862, and the hot season had begun. For two months there would be no rain, and almost no relief from the heat night or day. Even in the early morning the sun was a ball of fire. The Siamese steamer *Chow Phya* had come to anchor at the mouth of the river Chow Phya, and a troupe of circus performers was at the rails, trying to catch the first glimpse of the country whose king had invited them to entertain his family. Their trained dogs were barking and snarling at the two dogs that belonged to the captain of the ship.

Nearby, an Englishwoman was also leaning against the rail. Her lavender dress had a neat high collar and wrist-length sleeves. She was slender and graceful as she stood there with the breeze ruffling her full skirts. Chestnut curls framed a face that was pretty except for the rather prominent nose. As she looked across the water to the distant shore, a carefully dressed boy of about six came up from below deck, followed by a Hindustani nurse. His brown eyes danced and his brown hair was curly.

"Mama, Mama!" he cried. "Are we there?"

She turned to him with a smile. "Yes, we're there, Louis. In a little while we'll be in Bangkok. Shall we not, Captain Orton?" She addressed her question to the bronzed young man in uniform who had stepped up behind her son.

"We'll go in with the tide," the officer answered, "and you'll sleep on shore tonight."

Louis ran shouting with the news to the circus performers. "Stay with them, Beebe," the woman in lavender directed the nurse.

"Beebe takes good care of you, doesn't she?" asked the Captain.

The woman smiled, her eyes on the back of the nurse. "Beebe and her husband, Moonshee, have been with me since I was a girl," she said. "Louis and I couldn't do without them."

Captain Orton stood silent for a moment. A puff of fresh wind blew the woman's curls back. "Mrs. Leonowens," he said in a low voice, "a maid and an old Persian professor aren't enough. I don't like your going in there. Forgive me for saying so, but you can't even imagine what it's going to be like."

"You forget that I've lived in the East ever since I was fifteen."

"Yes, but in British colonies with British soldiers to protect you. This is Siam!"

The woman bit her lip. "I can't go back now. I've given my word to the King." The Captain turned away abruptly, but halfway down the deck he wheeled and came back. "I'll be in port every month. If you ever need me, the *Chow Phya* and I are at your service." He was gone without waiting for a reply.

The sun was very hot now. Sighing, the English-woman went below.

Anna had been born in Wales on November 5, 1834, and given the name Anna Harriette Crawford. When she was six her father, an army officer, had been ordered to India, and her mother had gone with him, leaving Anna behind in school. Before she was seven she was told that her father had died a soldier's death in his service to the Queen.

Eight years later she sailed to India to join her mother, who had married again. This fact changed the entire course of Anna's life. She was taken out to dinner parties for the first time. She went sight-seeing with her mother. She saw the wealth and poverty, the

3

grandeur and squalor of a strange world she could never have imagined. Most important of all, she fell in love with a young British officer, Major Thomas Louis Leonowens. They were married two years later, in 1851, and for a year they were very happy. Then a series of calamities began. Their first baby, a little girl, lived only a few months and then died. Anna's mother, to whom she was deeply attached, died at almost the same time.

Grief drove the young couple back to England, where Anna slowly healed and eventually bore two children—Avis and Louis Thomas. In 1856, Leon was ordered to Singapore. While the family was living there, a revolution broke out in India. One after another the banks there failed, and Anna, whose fortune had been invested in them, found herself penniless. Her little family was suddenly dependent on Leon's salary, which had never been large.

Still misfortune was not through with them. A year later Leon and some of his brother officers organized a tiger hunt. It was the hot season and Anna begged him not to go, but he was fond of hunting and the preparations were all made. He teased Anna by saying that she would make a house pet of him, and promised to be back by the next night.

The tiger led the men on a long chase—it was nearly noon before they bagged it. To keep his promise

Leon would have to ride through the heat of the day. The other officers urged him to wait until the sun had gone down, but he laughed at them. He reached home as he had said he would, and dropped unconscious at his wife's feet.

All night long she knelt beside his bed praying. But when morning dawned and there was no change, she knew at last that he was dead.

At only twenty-five years of age, Anna had lived a lifetime already. She had lost her parents, her husband, a child, and her modest fortune. Here she was in a strange land with two small children to support—she, who had never been expected to earn her own living. Fortunately, she had a good education, and with the encouragement of friends, she opened a school for officers' children. The school failed. But word of it—and Anna's abilities—reached the Siamese consul to Singapore, who had been instructed by the King of Siam to hire an English governess for the royal children.

After long negotiations, Anna received a letter from the King himself:

> *English Era, 1862, 26th February.*
> *Grand Royal Palace, Bangkok.*
> *To Mrs. A. H. Leonowens:—*
> *Madam: We are in good pleasure, and satisfaction in heart, that you are in willingness to*

undertake the education of our beloved royal children. And we hope that in doing your education on us and on our children (whom English call inhabitants of benighted land) you will do your best endeavor for knowledge of English language, science, and literature, and not for conversion to Christianity; as the followers of Buddha are mostly aware of the powerfulness of truth and virtue, as well as the followers of Christ, and are desirous to have facility of English language and literature, more than new religions.

We beg to invite you to our royal palace to do your best endeavorment upon us and our children. We shall expect to see you here on return of Siamese steamer Chow Phya.

We have written to Mr. William Adamson, and to our consul at Singapore, to authorize to do best arrangement for you and ourselves.

Believe me
Your faithfully,
(Signed) S. S. P. P. Maha Mongkut.

On receiving the letter, Anna arranged for her daughter Avis to enter boarding school in England. A mere two weeks after that, she and Louis were in Bangkok.

THE KRALAHOME

In the early afternoon the *Chow Phya* began its slow and careful passage up the winding river. The reddish-brown water curved between banks of lush green. Monkeys swung from bough to bough. Birds flashed and piped among the thickets.

Anna and her son stood against the rail watching, fascinated by the strangeness of this new country. The nearer they came to the city, the more frequent were the houses, thatched with palm, the pyramids and marble temple spires and turrets of the larger buildings. When they saw rows of floating houses on

either side of them, they knew that they had entered the city of Bangkok itself. Anna took a sudden sharp breath. Ahead was the glamour of the approaching night, the darkness and mystery of the land to which she had come. And the thought filled her with dread.

The ship moved on into the gathering darkness, dropping anchor at last. A little farther up the river Anna could discern a long white wall over which she could see, tier on tier, the roofs of the Royal Palace. She stood looking at them, oblivious of the innumerable rafts, boats, canoes, gondolas, junks, and ships that filled the river, the pall of black smoke from the steamer and the roar of its engine. Here she was, and there was the Palace where she was soon to begin her work as a teacher.

The circus people were preparing to leave. Over the side of the ship went their bundles and trunks into small boats. Off went the dogs and off went the people. The hatches were opened. The cargo was unloaded. And still no one had come for Anna. She began to feel a little frightened and very forlorn.

Then out of the shadows flashed a long gondola, beautifully carved like a dragon, with torches reflected on the rows of wet paddles. On its deck was a small gilded cabin, hung with curtains, and in it lay a Siamese official on a carpet and cushions. A man crouched in front of him with a fan.

The official mounted the side of the *Chow Phya* with an air of unconcern. A length of rich red silk folded loosely about his body. His brown skin gleamed in the torchlight. He was followed by a dozen crawling attendants. At his appearance, all the crew members flung themselves onto the deck in humility. Only Anna, Beebe, and Beebe's Persian husband, Moonshee, were left standing. Moonshee, who was a scholarly, rather frail man, took one look at the figure in the red skirt and began to pray.

Anna, meanwhile, stood composedly and waited. The official, equally composed, also waited. Out of the shadows stepped Captain Orton.

"Mrs. Leonowens, may I present His Excellency, Chao Phya Sri Suriyawong, Prime Minister of the Kingdom of Siam? Your Excellency, Mrs. Anna Leonowens."

The Englishwoman bowed slightly. The torches flickered across the firmly modeled face of the Prime Minister. It was immediately clear to Anna that this Siamese noble compelled respect. He had about him an air of command and latent power.

He beckoned a young attendant, who addressed Anna in English:

"Are you the lady who is to teach the royal family?"

She inclined her head slightly. "I am."

"Have you friends in Bangkok?"

"I know no one in Bangkok at all."

There was a quick flow of the Siamese language after this. The Englishwoman could not know that the owner of the proud black eyes understood perfectly what she said. His face was without expression. The interpreter spoke to her again: "What will you do? Where will you sleep tonight?"

"I don't know," she replied, holding her voice steady by an effort of will. "I am a stranger here. But I understood from His Majesty's letter that a residence would be provided for me on my arrival. And he has been informed that we would arrive at this time."

The lord and his interpreter surveyed her. The lord spoke, the interpreter translated. "His Majesty cannot remember everything," he said. At this the Prime Minister strode off and down the gangway, followed by his entourage. The dragon boat with its flickering torches and flashing paddles disappeared into the night.

Anna Leonowens was stunned by the rudeness of her reception.

"Do you see what I mean?" asked Captain Orton.

Anna was speechless.

Then a boat approached the *Chow Phya.* In a moment it was at the gangway.

"Captain Orton?" came a cheerful shout, and a jovial Englishman with graying hair and a round, ruddy face climbed aboard.

"Captain Bush!" exclaimed Orton. "What brings you here?"

"I just thought I'd drop around to greet you," replied the Englishman, who was Bangkok's harbor master. He bowed to Anna and introduced himself. On hearing of her plight, Bush instantly volunteered to help—he would be happy to look after Mrs. Leonowens until the King sent for her, most happy indeed.

Louis, half asleep, Beebe and Moonshee, the trunks and boxes, and last of all Anna herself were soon in the boat with Captain Bush. Captain Orton waved them away, shouting farewells and best wishes. Four men leaned on the oars and the small craft shot out into the dark river. The *Chow Phya*, Anna's last connection to home, faded from sight.

Under the steady sweep of the oars the boat moved through a dreamlike scene: high ships with lofty prows, tapering and elaborately curved, pretty little gondolas and canoes that passed continually. The fairy-like boats and the singing river soothed Anna.

In half an hour they drew up at a small landing and the tired little group climbed out. The boatmen unloaded the trunks and boxes. They straggled across a sandy yard, smooth and clean, and up wooden steps to a veranda. Mrs. Bush stood waiting for them, a sleeping baby in her arms. Unruffled by the arrival of strangers, she welcomed them with a pleasant smile.

"It's wonderfully kind of you to have us," Anna said.

"Not at all. It's a pleasure," Mrs. Bush replied comfortably, leading Anna and Louis to a room furnished with white iron beds, white sheets, and a round white bolster. Then she arranged beds on her back veranda for Moonshee and Beebe.

Anna undressed Louis and got him into his sleeper. She laid him on the bed and pulled the net tight. Mrs. Bush had gone. Though she was ready for bed, Anna could not sleep. The strange scenes of the day chased each other in confusion across her mind. She was sadly discouraged by her reception and thought now that perhaps Captain Orton was right. Perhaps she was making a mistake. The Prime Minister's refusal to assume any responsibility for her welfare frightened her. Fear of the unknown kept her tossing and turning. At long last she drifted into a troubled sleep. When she awoke the dawn was climbing a low wall and creeping in through the half-opened windows.

THREE

"HELLO, SIR!"

Dressing quickly and combing her hair, Anna braced herself for the day ahead. She scrubbed her face vigorously, but a look in the mirror told her that no water and soap could wash away her expression of fear and loneliness. Louis awoke when he heard her stirring. His eyes were eager and questioning, his smile bright and rested. A sudden ray of sunshine caught in his soft hair.

"Mama, we're here! Where's the Palace, Mama? I want to see it. Can we see it today?"

She smiled and drew him to the window.

"Kneel down, Louis, and we'll ask our Heavenly Father to take care of us in this new place."

When they were ready, they went into the outer room where Mrs. Bush led them to a breakfast table set with fruits and tea. A servant brought bowls of steaming rice and soup. Captain Bush joined them.

"Well, well, and how are you?" he asked heartily. "Another day, eh? Do things look better this morning? Of course they do, of course they do."

"The real question is, what shall I do next?" said Anna uncertainly.

"Do!" cried the Captain. "Don't do anything. This is Siam. You mustn't be rushing out and doing things. The important point here is to be able to wait until things come to you. Don't worry! The King's paid for your passage. He'll demand your services in good time."

"But the King doesn't even know where I am," she objected.

"Of course he does. The King knows everything that goes on here. You didn't expect him to meet you personally, did you? No, no, of course not. The Kralahome will send for you in due time."

"The *who* will send for me?"

"The Kralahome. The Prime Minister who met

you on the ship yesterday. The most important man in the kingdom. Everybody calls him by his Siamese title. He'll send for you when he has decided what to do with you!"

Breakfast was hardly over when this prophecy came true. The Kralahome's boat drew up at the landing. The interpreter told her that she was to bring her servants and her luggage and come to his master's palace at once.

Packing was finished quickly, and the little party was soon stowed in the long swift boat.

"Good-bye. God be with you." The Captain waved, and the boat shot out into the river, which was even busier in the daylight. Boats of all sorts and sizes were darting back and forth. Big junks with staring eyes pulled at their anchors.

In about a quarter of an hour the Kralahome's boat had crossed the river and drawn up at a stone quay in a small canal. Staying close together, Anna in the lead, Beebe with Louis and Moonshee, the little party walked across the quay to a low gateway, which opened into a stone courtyard. Two stone mandarins of ferocious aspect, mounted on horses, guarded the entrance. Live sentries stood nearby, dressed in European uniforms but barefoot. On the right was the Kralahome's palace.

Awed, they climbed the stairs to the palace. They

moved softly, following the interpreter, through spacious carpeted salons. At the windows were luxurious draperies. Crystal candelabra hung from the ceilings. A superb vase of silver stood on a table inlaid with mother-of-pearl. Flowers of great variety and beauty filled every room.

They came at last to the audience chamber. Anna caught sight of a number of young girls peeping at them from behind the velvet curtains. A large group of male attendants crouched in the antechamber. Some were in the poor clothing of servants or slaves, others were handsomely dressed younger relatives of the Kralahome. There was a subdued bustle of excitement, the peering of many dark eyes. And the little party of foreigners stood in the middle of it, wholly bewildered by the magnificence and strangeness of what they had seen.

Suddenly the curtains parted and the Kralahome stood before them. The murmuring ceased instantly. A wave of unreasoning fear overwhelmed Anna. She gritted her teeth. This man was powerful, and what he decided would affect all her future life. She found herself unable to think clearly. In all that room there was not a friendly face. In all Siam there was no one whom she could ask for help. She fought an impulse to run away.

The Kralahome held out his hand. "Good morning,

sir," he said in careful English. "Take a seat, sir."

She grasped the outstretched hand, and smiled involuntarily at the "sir."

"Thank you," she said, and sat down a little stiffly on a carved bench.

The noble approached her with an expression of pleased curiosity, and patted her small son on the head.

An interpreter crouched beside Anna on the floor. "Will you ask your master if he will please present my request for a quiet house or apartment to His Majesty as soon as possible?" she asked. "I should like to settle my belongings before my work begins. The King has promised me a residence near the Palace."

When this request was interpreted to the Kralahome, he stood smiling. After a careful study of her face and person he spoke directly to her in English. "You are not married?"

She bowed slightly. "My husband is dead."

Her answer seemed to puzzle the Kralahome. He began to pace up and down as if to solve by motion something that was not easily understood. What would a woman without a husband want with a house? Women in the East never lived alone, but always under the patronage of some male relative who gave them protection, fed, and clothed them. Finally he seemed to give up the riddle, or reach some decision, for he said something to his attendants.

Five or six of them raised themselves on their knees with their eyes fixed on the carpet and crawled backward until they reached the steps. They bobbed their heads and shoulders, started to their feet, and fled from the chamber.

There were more harsh words, and another half dozen of the slaves arose and ran. The Kralahome paced back and forth, carefully keeping an eye on Anna and Louis.

So they sat for half an hour, until Louis whispered, "Take me home, Mama!" Lowering his voice, he added, "I don't like that man."

Hearing this, the Kralahome stared at Louis, who clutched his mother's dress in terror. Anna was almost as frightened as Louis, but managed to maintain her control.

Another half hour went by, and the interpreter finally returned. He came across the floor on all fours, pushing one elbow out before the other as he crept along. As he reached his master he made an abject bow. There were a few unintelligible sentences. The Kralahome bowed, turned, disappeared behind a mirror.

The interpreter stood up and yawned.

"Hello. Good morning. How are you?" he said. "I am the Kralahome's half brother. Follow me, please. Rooms have been prepared for you."

The little group followed him down long and beautiful corridors. There was again the bewildering collection of statues and vases, Persian rugs, flowers, and then they were entering two large rooms. Their boxes and trunks had already been brought from the boat and were disposed around the wall. The room opened on a quiet piazza, shaded by fruit trees in blossom, and overlooked a small artificial lake stocked with colored fish.

Hardly had the Kralahome's half brother disappeared when the ladies of the Kralahome's harem descended in force. Crowding in through Anna's door, they all tried to embrace her affectionately, chattering in Siamese.

The youngest were hardly more than fourteen years of age. All were dressed in rich materials, although the fashion of their clothes did not differ from that of their slaves, numbers of whom were behind them prostrate on the floor of the room and down the halls outside.

One old woman shuffled through the noisy throng with an air of authority and, pointing to Louis, who had taken refuge in his mother's lap, cried in the familiar syllables of the Malay language, *"Moolay, moolay!"* (Pretty, pretty.) Anna had not heard Malay since her time in Singapore, and the familiar words fell pleasantly on her ears. She addressed the woman in Malay: "It is good to hear the Malay language again. But how does a Malay woman happen to be here in a Siamese palace?"

Instantly the visitors stopped their chatter and waited with interest. The old woman settled herself comfortably on a couch.

"Sixty years ago," she began, "my sister and I were working in the fields one day when we were captured by a party of Siamese adventurers. We were brought to Bangkok and sold for slaves, along with many other Malay girls who had been taken in the same way. At first I mourned my father and mother. But I was young and beautiful then, and I had been bought for the household of the Somdet Ong Yai, the father of my lord, the Kralahome. The prince noticed me, and I became his favorite. I bore him two lovely sons just as beautiful as this *moolay, moolay* boy. But they are dead. Alas, they are dead!" She wiped her eyes with the end of a silk scarf. Anna felt a quick surge of pity. She, too, knew the anguish of lost children. How alike women were everywhere!

"And my gracious lord is dead also. See, he gave me this beautiful gold betel box!"

Anna admired the box with a smile. "But how is it that you are still a slave?" she asked.

"Now I guard these favored ones," said the woman,

indicating the girls who surrounded her.

Her story ended, the old woman extracted some betel from her box and leaned back comfortably to chew it. The younger women, who had been quiet throughout, swarmed around Anna like bees, plying her with questions, which the old Malay translated.

"How old are you?"

"Have you a husband?"·

"Have you more children than this little boy?"

"What country do you come from?"

"Why did you come here?"

She answered patiently, trying to explain her position to them. They could not understand a woman who had come to a foreign country to work for her living. They had never known a woman who was not attached to some man as his mother, or his aunt, his wife, his daughter, his niece, his ward, or his slave. She laughed at the earnest eyes around her, and said: "You see, I am not like you. I must work to support my two children since my husband is dead. My daughter Avis is on the ocean going far away from me to England to school. She is a little girl only seven years old, and I am very sad now that I must be separated from her."

Sympathy flitted across the faces pressed close to hers. However strange Anna seemed to them, they understood instantly her pain at being separated from her child. Softly repeating, *"Phutho, Phutho!"* (Dear Buddha, dear Buddha!) they left her. A minute more and she heard them laughing as they retreated down the corridors of the palace.

FOUR

AN EXOTIC
HOUSEHOLD

After her visitors had gone, Anna began to unpack. The apartment was comfortably furnished with chests, beds, wardrobes, and chairs from Singapore and Hong Kong. Louis was happily playing in the little garden near the pond while Beebe kept guard. Suddenly all the weariness of the day before overcame Anna. She lay down on the bed, grateful for the quiet of the spacious rooms, and fell into a deep and dreamless sleep.

Anna woke and continued unpacking until five o'clock, when two dark-eyed little boys, weighed down by their heavy brass trays, arrived with dinner. So it was that she and Louis began, rather uncertainly, their first Siamese meal. It was a mixture of European foods—boiled vegetables and roast chicken prepared especially for them—and Siamese curries and rice. After tasting everything, even the curries, Louis pronounced the food good, and Anna agreed. They finished their meal with a dessert of mangoes and bananas.

The pages watched them with great interest, whispering and giggling as Anna and Louis ate their fruit using forks and knives. Anna shook her head at them, but if they understood that she wished them to leave, they gave no sign. Instead they hovered until Anna and Louis put down their silverware, and then launched into an acrobatic show of handstands and somersaults which Louis viewed with his mouth hanging open in astonishment.

Then they stopped suddenly and flew out of the room. Anna resolved to press the King for a house of her own right away.

The next morning she answered a knock at the door, and found a Eurasian man standing there.

"I am Mr. Robert Hunter, ma'am. His Excellency's secretary. Is there anything that I can do to help you?"

"Mr. Hunter, I am so glad to meet you. I don't need anything now," said Anna, "but I shall certainly be calling upon you for help later."

He bowed gravely. "My duties as harbor officer quite frequently take me out for many hours of the day, but I am always in for at least a while." His manner of speaking was stilted but friendly. "I shall be delighted to be of service. If there is nothing you want now, I shall be going."

"Do you have any idea when the King will send for me, Mr. Hunter?"

"It's hard to say, ma'am. It may be several days or several weeks. His Majesty is busy with two important ceremonies, which started the day you came here and will last until the twenty-first. He is raising his oldest son, Prince Chulalongkorn, to official rank. The boy is to be presented with a gold tablet engraved with his royal name. And then he's to be invested with official position and title."

"You mean he's to be installed as crown prince?" Anna asked with interest.

"Well, no, not exactly that. There isn't any such office. But he will have a grade of forty thousand *sakdina*. I hardly know how to translate it, but a common man has only six *sakdina*—ranks or points you might call it—so naturally forty thousand will place him above everyone else in the kingdom. In a way it does make him the same as the crown prince."

"And will he be one of my pupils?"

"I think he will," Mr. Hunter assured her.

Anna was pleased with this news.

The anti-slavery movement in the United States had moved her deeply. Perhaps the opportunity to teach here meant that she would be able to convey to her pupils the sacredness of the human soul, and the evil of any system which violated it by permitting one person to own another. If the young heir was to be her pupil she could hope, at least, to mold him a little. All this flashed through her mind as she asked Mr. Hunter: "And you think I'll be sent for as soon as the ceremony is over?"

"It's impossible to say, ma'am," he said. "New Year starts on the twenty-ninth and there is always a great to-do with fireworks on the river and on the royal plaza, and theatricals in all the palaces. And His Majesty is getting ready for the public cremation of his late queen consort, Prince Chulalongkorn's mother, who died last September. That will be in April sometime and will take a week or two. I think you may count on having some time to yourself." He bowed again and left.

Shortly after, a page came with a card which read, "Mr. George Orton." Behind him was the Captain, smiling. Anna was quite pleased to see him.

"We're sailing with the tide," he explained. "And I wanted to ask you if you had anything to send back to your friends in Singapore."

"Captain Orton, how kind of you! Do sit down. Will I have time to send Beebe out for fruit?" Learning that he could wait, she dispatched Beebe at once. "Get some pomelos, Beebe, and mangoes, if you can."

While he waited, she sat down and wrote a letter to Avis. Tears came to her eyes as she sealed it and handed it over to the Captain, with the basket of fruit for her Singapore friends. He held her hand for a moment as he asked, "You're staying, then?"

"I'm staying," she said in a low voice.

"God bless you," he said, and was gone.

The unpacking was harder than ever after that. Anna could not stop thinking of the daughter she had sent away. She felt the little arms around her neck as they had been that last day in Singapore, when she was about to leave for the *Chow Phya*. "Mama, Mama, I won't let you go," Avis had said. And Anna had thought herself very cruel as she removed herself from her daughter's embrace and entrusted the small soft body to strangers—friends, yes, but strangers nonetheless.

How long she sat there she did not know. A knock at the door aroused her. A Siamese woman entered. She was perhaps forty, stout, dark, heavy of feature. She was followed by a large retinue, which proclaimed her the chief woman in this establishment filled with women. She took Anna's hands between her own gently as the old Malay woman of the day before interpreted.

"This is Khun Ying Phan," she said, "head wife of the Kralahome. She bids you welcome and asks if there is anything that you will need."

"Thank her for me, and invite her to be seated."

The Khun Ying took a seat upon one of the low sofas, bringing her feet up and behind her. "Are you comfortable here?" she asked through the old woman.

"Please tell her that I'm quite comfortable and also that I am grateful to her for these pleasant apartments and the good meals her servants have been bringing me and my son."

The Khun Ying looked gratified at the praise of her meals. "How many children have you, Mem?" she asked.

"I have two, a girl and a boy. The girl is on her way to England to school."

The Khun Ying's face showed sympathy. "Ah, that is hard, that is hard indeed."

"Offer her some gift, Mem," prompted the old woman.

Anna selected from a basket a little pair of scissors of which she was fond. "Will Lady Phan accept this small gift as a token of my appreciation of her hospitality?"

Lady Phan was enchanted with the gift, turning it over and over in her palm. One handle was delicately fashioned like a stork. "Some day soon you must come and see my garden," she said.

"I have noticed the lovely flowers in vases in every room in the palace."

The Khun Ying smiled again, pleased. And now that her business was over, she went on with the business of the palace, which kept her occupied from dawn till dark.

FIVE

AN AUDIENCE
WITH THE KING

The weather began to be very hot. As one stifling day after another dragged itself out, Anna waited more and more impatiently for her interview with the King. But no summons came, nor did she get any word that a house had been prepared for her.

Morning and evening she and Louis strolled in the garden or out to the river's edge. Sometimes Anna called on Khun Ying Phan. Her house was in the women's quarters and was beautifully furnished with

antique Siamese furniture, sofa beds, low couches, tables, and a few chairs. There was nothing foreign in the houses, not even carpets or mirrors. There was an air about the house of coolness and repose, despite the hot March sun that shone along the satin floor through silken window nets.

Around the house bloomed an equally charming garden. There were flowering trees, ferns, and shrubs. A cool, shaded walk ran to an even larger garden, bordered with lattice work, and filled with flowering shrubs of extraordinary beauty.

"These flowers are the children of my heart," said the Khun Ying, as she and Anna walked there. And then in a whisper, "For as you know, my lord is childless."

But the Khun Ying had little time to spare for visiting. More than a thousand of the prince's retainers lived around the palace and within it. There were also several hundred slaves to be directed. This miniature city was the Khun Ying's responsibility.

As the days passed, Anna grew to admire her more and more. She was mild in her manner, but very efficient. The big establishment moved easily with the same calm as its mistress. Anna was especially impressed with her kindness to the younger women of her husband's harem. She lived among them as happily as if they were her daughters. She shared their confidences and comforted their sorrows and pleaded their cause with her lord and theirs. She even managed to exercise a cautious influence over the Kralahome himself, in spite of his cold and unyielding appearance.

On the fateful afternoon of April 3, Anna dressed with special care. Over her mauve muslin dress she wore a black lace shawl from the India days. After several weeks of negotiations with the Kralahome, it had been decided that she should be presented at court by Captain John Bush, the harbor master.

With her best bonnet framing the smooth brown curls around her face, Anna waited with Louis, who had refused to stay behind. Scrubbed, groomed, and wearing his best jacket, he was ready to accompany his mother.

Promptly at five o'clock Captain Bush arrived, puffing a little in his high-necked suit, but ruddy and cheerful as always. The little party moved out of the canal and across the river in his boat. Louis, miserable in the unrelenting heat, was silent. Once he leaned against his mother and whispered, "Mama, I'm afraid of the King!"

"There's nothing to be afraid of, dear," she whispered back, willing herself to believe it. "You've never even seen him."

But a spasm of fear squeezed her own heart at the prospect of the interview with the strange King, about whom she had heard so many sinister things. She must make just the right impression on this mysterious ruler, whom his subjects called "the Lord of Life." The only question was how.

She puzzled over this as the boat moved steadily across the river to the Palace landing. It was teeming with activity. A large party of priests were bathing in the river. Other priests, standing on the bank in wet yellow robes, were wringing out garments they had just finished washing. Graceful girls with vessels of water balanced on their heads were passing along the road that bordered the quay, while others carried bundles of hay or baskets of fruit. Noblemen in gilded sedans, borne on the backs of sweating slaves, were hurrying toward the late afternoon audience. In the distance Anna caught a glimpse of a troop of spearmen, the sun glittering on their long weapons.

Captain Bush, Anna, and Louis climbed out of the boat and walked through the covered gangway of the landing to a clean brick road, which took them away from the river and down a narrow street bounded on either side by high brick walls.

They turned left with the palace wall and came to the Wat Phra Keo, Temple of the Emerald Buddha, most fabulous of all the gorgeous temples of Siam, and the King's private chapel.

Beyond the temple they passed into a paved court-yard. The fantastic roofs of palaces and still more temples, soaring tier on tier, sparkled and gleamed. A short walk brought them to the Amarind Palace. They paused uncertainly at the entrance, but there was no one waiting to guide them, so they walked in unescorted. They passed through several ante-chambers until they came to the Audience Hall itself.

A flood of late afternoon sunlight swept through the spacious hall from high windows, upon a throng of noblemen dressed in gold-encrusted silks of various colors. All were crouched on their elbows and knees with their heads down, facing the golden throne at the far end. On it sat the King. He was of medium height and very thin, dressed in what seemed to be cloth of gold. As he sat cross-legged and motionless, he appeared to have been carved of a piece of the glittering throne.

The little group on the steps waited and watched for perhaps five minutes, but, when it appeared that no one intended to pay them the slightest attention, Anna whispered to Captain Bush, "Please do present us at once. Louis is beginning to be quite tired and hungry."

"Better to wait, ma'am," said Captain Bush.

But Anna's patience was exhausted. She took Captain Bush by the arm and together they mounted the steps with Louis, entering the hall unannounced. Ranged on the deep red carpet were the prostrate, mute, motionless forms of hundreds of courtiers and noblemen.

The King caught sight of them at once. He sprang to his feet and advanced rapidly down the length of the hall. "Who? Who?" he demanded.

When he reached them, Captain Bush, on his knees like the other courtiers, said, "Your Majesty, the new English governess, Mrs. Anna Harriette Leonowens, and her son, Louis."

Anna curtsied deeply, and then balanced herself as best she could with bent knees in the froglike position she had been told would be acceptable.

The King shook hands with her, watching her all the while with dark, shrewd eyes. But he said nothing at all. With his appraising eyes still on her, he began to march up and down the carpet in front of her in quick steps. He put one foot before the other with mathematical precision, as if bent on accurately performing the steps of some intricate drill. His feet were encased in gold slippers turned up at the toe and crusted with gems that refracted little gleams of light as he moved.

Captain Bush whispered out of the corner of his

mouth, "The fireworks'll begin in a minute, ma'am. Best to be prepared!"

Suddenly the King took one long final stride and brought himself to a halt exactly in front of Anna at a distance of three feet. He stretched his arm at full length and pointed his forefinger at her nose.

"How old shall you be?" he asked.

Anna was taken completely by surprise. In all her worrying over his interview she had never imagined it beginning like this. She was hardly able to suppress a smile. Yet she was annoyed, too, at the prospect of a cross-examination into her private life in front of the hundreds of kneeling men. Such personal questions should have been asked before she was employed or in private. Still, she did not wish to offend the King. She thought quickly and answered demurely, "One hundred and fifty years old, Sire."

The pointing hand dropped. Surprised and puzzled, the King resumed his march, back and forth, back and forth, in quick, even steps. His jet eyes scrutinized her face, then lit up with understanding. He coughed, laughed, coughed, and returned to the attack. "In what year were you borned?"

With a grave and serious expression she replied, "I was born in 1712, Your Majesty."

The expression on the King's face was indescribably funny. Captain Bush, who had begun to rumble ominously, slipped behind a pillar to laugh undetected. The King coughed with a significant emphasis that startled Anna. Was he angry with her for her boldness in evading his questions? Then he addressed a few quick words to the nearest courtiers, who smiled at the carpet beneath their noses—all but the Kralahome, who turned and studied her, frowning.

In the meantime the King had taken up his quick march again, studying Anna's face as if he were learning it by heart. Then he stopped, wheeled, and lunged. "How many years shall you be married?"

"For several years, Your Majesty," returned the new governess. She was determined not to be outwitted, and not to reveal any of the facts of her private life in this public place unless they dealt with her qualifications as a governess. She had begun to enjoy the battle, which was like a child's game of wooden swords.

The King took six steps, paused, and fell into a deep silence. After several minutes of careful thought he turned again. Then he rushed at her and demanded triumphantly, "Ha! How many grandchildren shall you have by now? Ha, Ha! How many? How many? Ha, ha, ha!"

Everyone laughed heartily, including Anna. It was clear that the King, in his own way, had accepted her.

Now he seized Anna's hand and dragged her

rapidly down the length of the Audience Hall past the ranks of kneeling men and through a curtained door at the back. Louis clung desperately to her skirt. They flew along a succession of covered passages. When Anna and Louis were quite out of breath the King stopped at last before one of a series of curtained recesses. He pushed open the velvet hangings.

There on the floor was the kneeling form of a woman whose face was covered with her scarf. The King drew aside the pleated silk. Her features were delicate and very beautiful. Stooping, he took her hand and placed it in the one of Anna's that he still held. It rested there, unresisting as a timid bird.

"This is my wife, the Lady Talap," said the King. "She desires to be educated in English. She has had some lessons from the ladies of the mission. And she is as pleasing for her talent as for her beauty. It is our pleasure to make her a good English scholar. You shall educate her for us."

Something about the young woman won over Anna completely. Her modest and gentle bearing was very charming. "That would give me a great pleasure, Your Majesty," Anna said.

As the King translated the reply to Lady Talap, she laughed in a clear ripple of sound like temple bells. She cast in Anna's direction a look of such genuine joy that Anna was startled. Was it so much to ask, to study English? The Lady Talap apparently thought it was. She appeared so enraptured with the graciousness of the King's act, so overjoyed at the granting of her wish as she knelt before them, that Anna left her with a mingled feeling of affection and pity.

The King led her back through the corridors toward the great hall. Dozens of children had come out of the inner precincts of the Palace. The King addressed them indulgently, but it was Louis who attracted them. They descended upon him, chattering, laughing, and shouting. He pulled back shyly as they reached out to touch him, but they only pressed closer. They fingered his clothing, his hair, his skin, his shoes, and his strange white hands. Louis looked beseechingly at Anna, but there was nothing she could do except keep on walking. The King laughed.

"I have sixty-seven children," he said proudly, as they reached the Audience Hall, and Louis was free at last. "You shall educate them for me, and as many of my wives also as wish to learn English. And I have much correspondence in which you must assist me." Leaning closer to her, he went on, "And, moreover, I have much difficulty for reading and translating French letters, for French are fond of using gloomily deceiving terms. You must undertake, and you shall make all their murky sentences and gloomily deceiving propositions clear to me. And, furthermore, I have by every mail foreign letters whose writing is not easily read by me. You shall copy on round hand for my easily review thereof."

Anna was appalled at the prospect of her duties, but thought it best to keep quiet for the time being.

"I will send for you later," the King finished with a wave of his hand. Anna curtsied, and even Louis managed a bob of the head. Then they withdrew with Captain Bush and were shortly out in the evening air.

Anna breathed deeply, profoundly thankful to be outside the Palace walls.

"I'm tired, Mama," said Louis.

She took his hand. "So am I, dearest."

SIX

THE
ROYAL TEMPER

While she waited for the King's summons to start the school, Anna decided to study the Siamese language. Mr. Hunter supplied her with a teacher, a withered old man who had once been a priest.

After a week of lessons she was able to begin halting conversations with the women of the harem. These were limited to words and the simplest sentences— "Are you well?" "What do you call this?" and so on. The women entered into the new game with enthusiasm. They told her the names of all the objects in her room, and she pronounced the words after them.

Her memory was good, and she soon knew many common nouns, adjectives, and verbs. She began to be able to detect here and there a word when it was spoken rapidly in ordinary conversation. Once in a while she understood an entire sentence. The fascination which language always held for her made the dull, hot days interesting.

Finally one morning Mr. Hunter came from the Kralahome to tell her to be prepared to begin her duties at the Palace at once.

"The Kralahome's sister, Lady Piam, will take you," he said. "She'll call for you tomorrow morning with her boat."

Early the next day Lady Piam appeared at Anna's door. She was a broad, motherly woman whose greeting was as warm as her smile. "Good morning, sir," she said to Anna.

"Good morning," replied Anna. "It's kind of you to come for me. Shall we start at once?"

"Good morning, sir," answered Lady Piam. Taking this to mean yes, Anna put on her cloak, bonnet, and gloves. Louis, who had insisted on coming along, put on his hat and picked up his schoolbooks. Calling good-bye to Beebe, he followed Anna and Lady Piam.

After the party was seated in the covered basket boat, Lady Piam caught sight of Louis's books and picked one up with interest. When, in turning over the pages, she came upon the alphabet, she gave Anna a look of pleased surprise and started to say the letters, pointing at each with her finger. Anna helped her, and for a while she seemed gratified and amused. But a short time later she closed the book abruptly and offered Anna her plump hand, saying, "Good morning, sir."

Anna replied, "Good morning," and after a moment's thought added "sir."

The boat proceeded in a leisurely fashion up the river, landing at an ancient, dilapidated pavilion that jutted into the water. They went through several covered passages to a barrier guarded by Amazons. These were strongly built women, a little taller than Anna, with very short hair which was the usual style of the country. They wore tight-fitting jackets of scarlet buttoned to the neck, with sashes tied diagonally across their chests. Their lower garments were a sort of plaid that reminded Anna of kilts. Lady Piam was evidently well known to them, for they threw open the door quickly and then squatted with their hands folded before their faces until she and her party had passed.

A hot walk of twenty minutes brought the party to the inner wall, which shut off the harem, called the Inside, from the rest of the Palace grounds. A strange oval door of polished brass opened noiselessly to admit them to the courtyard.

On their left were several lofty temples set among groves of old trees; on their right was a long, dim gallery. The floor of the open pavilion on which they walked was marble. The shade from the trees and the coolness of the room were a relief after the heat of the day.

A number of women lounging in and around the pavilion started up to greet Lady Piam. When the formalities were over, they all fell into animated conversation. Children sat or sprawled upon the marble floor. Babies slept or played in the arms of their nurses.

Almost immediately slaves appeared with silver trays. These were covered with scarlet netting stretched over light frames of bamboo, in the shape of beehives. After the beehives were removed, Anna saw that the trays were filled with strange and appetizing foods. Anna would have liked to try them, but no forks or spoons were provided and she could not bring herself to use her fingers, as the others did. She and Louis had to content themselves with oranges.

When Anna and Louis began to peel the fruit, the children came close to watch. They laughed and pointed and talked, though she and Louis could not imagine what was so odd about the way they were eating. Later she learned that the Siamese peeled all fruit with the knife pointed away from themselves and considered foreigners indescribably foolish for cutting toward their own thumbs. The children were attractive, with soft brown skin, liquid brown eyes, and well-formed bodies. But when Anna had finished her orange and held out her hand to them, they drew away.

Soon Lady Talap, who had so charmed Anna at their first meeting, appeared. After saluting the sister of the Kralahome with great respect, and talking with her for a few minutes, she beckoned to Anna, smiling with the sudden sweetness that distinguished her from the other women. Anna got up and went over to her. As she sat down beside the pretty, relaxed figure, Lady Talap said in quiet, clear English, "I am very glad to see you. It is long time I not see. Why you come so late?" to all of which she apparently expected no reply. Anna replied with several simple sentences, but Lady Talap shook her head, laughing.

They sat together as the day wore on to noon. Some women went, others came. The children continued to play. Anna felt as if she had fallen into an enchanted world out of an old fairy tale. It seemed impossible that only twenty minutes' walk could bring her to the outer stir and bustle of Bangkok.

A slight noise suddenly came from the covered gallery. An old woman appeared, bearing a candlestick of gold. The effect was instantaneous and amazing.

All the drowsy laziness of the afternoon vanished. Lady Talap started to her feet and fled. The other women and even most of the children followed suit. Anna was left alone with the Kralahome's sister and her attendants, and Louis, who was sleeping comfortably in his mother's lap.

It was easy to guess that the King was in some way connected with the candles. Later, when she understood the customs of palace life, Anna learned that the candlestick was the offering the King sent to the Chapel Royal of Wat Phra Keo as soon as he awakened from his nap; and it meant that his appearance was imminent.

In a few minutes a straggling procession began to move past—hundreds of women and children, all walking quietly in one direction. Anna began to feel uneasy. All this hushed and careful bustle made her uneasy. She determined to take up with the King personally the question of a house. He had promised her a brick house in his letter, but as the Kralahome had said on that first, unforgettable night, "His Majesty cannot remember everything." Perhaps he needed to be reminded.

She took out the two letters from the King that had come to Singapore, and reread them. In addition to the letter which had been addressed to her personally, she had a copy of the King's letter to Mr. W. Tan Kim Ching, which was very specific:

Bangkok, 26th. Feb. 1862

In regard to the Lady whose name you have said Mrs. Leonowens whom you pleased mostly to have in our employ for being school mistress here, if the Lady Leonowens accept to receive salary for every month but $100 and promise to live in this palace or in vicinity hereof, and that she will do education of language and literature more than endeavour to convert our Children to Christ religion I shall be glad to have her our school Mistress according to your favourable opinion.

I have written to Mr. Wm. Adamson who and whose wife have introduced the application of this Lady to you before, on this subject and have ordered him that the said Lady shall place good arrangement with you before she would come up here. I beg to authorize for doing best arrangement with her who may be not out of my aforesaid rules.

When she would come up here I will give her a brick house in nearest vicinity of this palace where she can live with her husband or manservants freely without rent or lessening payment the monthly salary will be $100 firstly—but afterwards when I observe her labour greater than expected or her scholars will be increased or her scholars may become in facility of language and literature very soon, I will reward her some time more than salary or *add her monthly salary according to her labour.*

Please state my statement to her, and let her believe me.

She folded the letters away again and aroused Louis. The straggling procession of women and children had stopped. She stood up to await the King.

She would not admit to herself that she was afraid of him, yet she was very tense and nervous.

There was a general frantic rush. Nurses and slaves vanished through doors, around pillars, under stairways. And at last, preceded by a sharp cough, the King himself appeared. He was not smiling. He approached the pavilion coughing loudly and, it seemed to Anna, crossly. Louis buried his face in the folds of his mother's dress to escape the notice of this person who announced himself so strangely. The trail of women and children following the King prostrated themselves as he paused before the Kralahome's sister. She, too, had dropped to the floor. Only the English-woman and her child were left standing.

The King shook hands with Anna. He then turned to the Kralahome's sister and talked with her for a long time. Anna waited, but he paid no further attention to her. As she waited, several of the women inched closer to her and hissed something at her. She could not understand them, and so remained with her eyes fixed on the King's face, trying to guess what he was saying to Lady Piam.

It was not a handsome face, although the features were regular and the complexion smooth. But it was a strong face and a shrewd one, the face of a man who was used to having his own way.

The hissing of the women resumed. Anna looked down at them curiously, but their eyes were on the ground as they squatted on their elbows and knees. She wondered what they were trying to say to her. Evidently they considered it important enough to run the risk of a rebuke from their lord. Didn't they know that she couldn't understand them?

They said nothing more, but suddenly without warning four of them reached out and took hold of her skirt. Before she could guess what they intended to do, they had pulled together vigorously. The movement was so quick that she lost her balance. Triumphantly they jerked her over backward and she landed full length on the pavement, stunned, with Louis lying beside her. Tears of pain and anger came to her eyes. Furiously she attempted to struggle to her feet, but they held tight until the King saw her dilemma. He spoke rapidly, and Anna was allowed to resume her upright position, rumpled and shaken.

"They not understand English custom of standing in presence of royalty," said the King, as Anna tried to smooth her dress and soothe Louis.

The King spoke to the women and again they crawled backward a little and left Anna alone on a small open space. Then with a wave of his hand the King said, "It is our pleasure that you shall reside within this Palace among our family."

Only half recovered from the shock of the fall, Anna was struck dumb. Live here? How could she live here? She would have no privacy and no freedom to come and go! Every gate was guarded and every movement of those within watched. She wanted a home not only for herself but also for Louis. She closed her trembling lips firmly. She could never live here. Never, she decided, she would never consent.

"Your Majesty," she said with a quietness she did not feel, "it is impossible for me to live here. I shall be happy to work here during the school day, but I need a home outside the Palace where I can go when my duties are done. I should feel like a prisoner when the Palace gates are shut in the evening."

The King looked at her suspiciously. "Where do you go every evening?"

"Not anywhere, Your Majesty," she replied indignantly. "I'm a stranger here."

"Then why shall you object to the gates being shut?"

"I hardly know," she answered slowly, "but I beg Your Majesty to remember that in your gracious letter you promised me a brick residence adjoining the Royal Palace, not within it."

The King took several quick steps toward her.

"I do not know I have promised. I do not know former condition. I do not know anything but you are my servant"—the voice was climbing higher—"and it is our pleasure that you must live in this Palace, *and you shall obey!*" The last three words were shouted at her.

She backed off a little, trembling. "If I give up now," she thought, "I'm lost." She gathered what was left of her courage and managed to say in a voice so calm that it surprised her, "Your Majesty has perhaps forgotten that I am not a servant, but a governess. I expect to obey Your Majesty's commands within the obligation of my duty to your family, but beyond that I can promise no obedience."

"You shall live in the Palace," he shouted. "You shall live in the Palace!" Then he blinked his eyes rapidly several times and spoke in an ordinary tone of voice. "I will give women slaves to wait on you. You shall commence royal school in this pavilion Thursday next. That is the best day for such undertaking in the estimation of our astrologers."

Anna drew a deep breath. Slaves! If he knew how she hated slavery and how she would do everything in her power to destroy it, he would not think she could be won over for a few pitiful human beings! The King turned away as if the matter were settled and began to issue commands to some old women crouching at the edge of the pavilion.

A sob came from Louis. The Kralahome's sister raised her head and threw him several fierce glances. Children were not permitted to cry in the presence of the King. Anna felt tears gathering in her own eyes. After all, who was she, one frail Englishwoman, to pit herself against this King? Still, she would not live in the Palace. And she had better not stay and burst into undignified tears. That would reveal her inner weakness, and here one could not afford to be weak. If she waited for the King to end the interview, she would surely break down and cry. It would be better to seem rude than weak. Taking Louis by the hand, she turned and walked quickly toward the brass door.

Voices behind her began to call. "Mem, Mem, Mem." The King was beckoning and shouting. The tears were close to the surface now and she was shaking. She bowed and hurried on through the oval door, head held high.

Lady Piam came after her in rage, tugging at Anna's cloak and crying, *"Mai di, mai di."* Anna knew enough Siamese to understand that simple phrase—"Bad, bad!" But she walked on, outwardly quiet, toward the gate that led to the river. She would not be bullied!

All the way up the river in the boat there were more *Mai di*'s and none of the "Good morning's" of the earlier trip. Even up to the very door of her room Lady Piam continued to pelt her with words she could not understand, mixed with *"Mai di, mai di, mai di."* But Anna's mind was made up. She could resign her position if she must! But she would not live in the Palace.

SEVEN

A HOME AT LAST

The more Anna thought, the more apparent it became to her that the unfortunate interview with the King could not have been avoided. He expected those about him to adapt themselves to his whims. This she could not and would not do. Still, she could hardly expect to get the better of the King without help. She must somehow enlist the aid of the Kralahome.

She decided to go to him at once and tell him what had happened. Already she felt his power in the kingdom. Those who came in contact with him both feared and loved him. The reason for the fear she had felt at their first meeting on shipboard. The reason for the respect and love he inspired she could not fathom, unless it came from his reputation for justice. He was known for a rigid sense of right and wrong.

As if in answer to her thought, Mr. Hunter knocked on her door and asked whether there was anything he could do for her.

"Oh, yes, Mr. Hunter, there is! I should like very much to speak with the Kralahome about what happened at the Palace this afternoon."

In a few minutes Mr. Hunter was back to say that the Kralahome would receive her in his private sitting room. He was smoking a pipe when Mr. Hunter ushered her in—sitting in front of a litter of papers in the Siamese language.

"Yes?" he said, looking up and taking the pipe out of his mouth.

"Your Excellency has heard of the interview this afternoon?"

A faint smile relieved the impassivity of his face. He nodded.

"Nothing was farther from my thoughts than such an unpleasant conversation with His Majesty. But it is impossible for me to live in the Palace." She drew out the two letters she had carried to the Palace with her and laid them before him. "I have accepted the King's terms and expect to fulfill my part of the bargain, but I feel strongly that His Majesty is bound in honor to keep his promise."

The Kralahome picked up the letters and read them carefully. When he put them down and looked at her she saw that she had succeeded in arousing his interest.

"What for you object to live in the Palace?"

How could she make him understand her need for privacy? It was something the Siamese did not seem to want or even to like. "Your Excellency," she began slowly, "my work will be difficult. It will take many hours, and when it is finished I shall be very tired indeed. I need a home where I can retire for the evening. And then, too, the Palace gates are shut early. As you know, Europeans do much of their visiting at the dinner table. I want to be free to entertain my friends in the usual way, and I couldn't do this in the Palace. I shall be happy to work there, and even to assume the duties of secretary that the King has decided to add to my schoolwork, but I feel that I'm entitled to a place to live where I shall be able to follow the customs of my own people without giving offense to anyone."

The Kralahome listened attentively, then asked several questions of Mr. Hunter in Siamese. "Very well, sir," he said to Anna.

Two months passed, and nothing happened. Finally, in desperation, Anna settled down to her studies in Siamese and Sanskrit. Then suddenly one afternoon the Kralahome paid her a visit, something he had not done before. He complimented her on her progress in Siamese and on her *Chai yai*, her "large-heartedness." He told her that the King had been angered by her conduct and that it was not possible to make any progress until His Majesty got over his annoyance.

Anna tried to conceal her disappointment but her voice faltered when she asked, "How . . . long do you think that will be? I would so like to begin teaching."

"Maybe long time. Maybe short time," said the Kralahome. Then he said, "Siamese lady like play. You like work. Why you no like play?"

Anna laughed ruefully. "I like play," she said, "but I like work also, and I am tired of being idle. Indeed, I am growing rather tired of Siam."

He received her frankness with a smile and a good-humored "Good-bye, sir."

As June became July Anna reflected on her un-equal struggle with the King. She had come to Siam believing deeply in the importance of human freedom.

She had dreamed of influencing the nation through its royal family. Perhaps, she had thought, by teaching some future king of Siam, she could shape his mind for a new and better world—a world without slavery.

Because of this dream, she had resisted the objections of her friends, who considered her venture wild and dangerous. Battles against slavery were best left to men with guns, they said, like the soldiers in the United States, not to frail Englishwomen! She hadn't a hope of opposing the ruler of a feudal country, surely she knew that! But Anna had been convinced that she could effect change here, and she had rejected their arguments.

Now, as the months passed, she felt her spirits sinking and her dreams fading away. There would be no modern education for the royal children of Siam. The King would make sure of that, just as he had made sure she had no living quarters of her own.

Then one morning the Kralahome's wife, Khun Ying Phan, walked into Anna's room unannounced. "Mem," she said, "I have found a house for you."

Anna sprang up, overcome with gratitude. She had told Lady Phan of her wish for a house of her own, but had never expected that the lady would find one for her. Now her heart almost burst with joy.

Lady Phan smiled and begged her not to expect too much. "But it is on the river and it has a small garden. You may have it if you like. Do you want to go and see it now?"

Anna was amazed to discover she could be happy again. She thanked Lady Phan for her kindness with so much enthusiasm that the Siamese woman laughed. A young brother of the Kralahome accompanied them, and they set off on foot, along with Louis, Beebe, and Moonshee.

After passing through several narrow alleys, they came at last to a walled enclosure. Inside, at the far end of the yard, stood the house. A picturesque wooden building with shuttered windows, it was shaded by several fine old trees. A door in the wall to the right of the house opened on the river, which glinted in the morning sun. Anna's spirits rose even higher.

When they toured the house they found nine rooms, including bathrooms and a kitchen. Some of the rooms were pleasant and airy; others were small and cozy. All were dirty, a fact which caused Moonshee to sigh loudly and frequently.

Except for the dirt the house was livable, and soap and water would help that. Beebe and Louis were very optimistic. Anna gave Moonshee a few dollars and packed him off to buy some buckets. Beebe tied an apron on Louis. He had announced that he would help clean while Beebe returned to the palace to pack their belongings. Without any discussion, they had all decided to stay.

Anna sat down on the only chair in the house, a broken one of Chinese design, to plan the attack. The first question was where to begin! There was so much dirt! After some thought she marched through a broken door into an inner room and began tearing up the rotted floor matting. After months of boredom there was sheer joy in the use of physical energy.

Moonshee returned with half a dozen buckets. He looked at the dirty walls and floors, and then sat down on the steps. But Anna refused to be discouraged.

"Get up, Moonshee!" she said. "Go and fetch Beebe. And you can bring the beds and boxes yourself while she helps me clean. We're going to clean at least two rooms, and we're going to stay. Come on, now, get up!" The old man looked at her sadly, stood up, and shuffled off.

By late afternoon the house was immaculate. New matting, which smelled like fresh hay, had been found and laid on the floor. The furniture was carried in and set in place. There was not enough of it for so big a house, but Anna did not care. There were a table and two armchairs. There were some candlesticks, and many books, which came out of their boxes like old friends. There was also a piano waiting to be played with the familiar songs they all enjoyed. In the bed-room Louis's cot had been spread with white sheets and set next to Anna's bed. Snowy white nets were ready to be lowered against the mosquitoes. On the table beside the bed Anna set a picture of Avis. That was the final touch.

It was quiet. There was only the lap of the river against the bank and the sound of some children splashing and swimming in it. Louis! Where was Louis? Anna and Beebe found him asleep on the floor in one of the empty rooms. They carried him to his bed and laid him on it. Then Anna washed and put on her muslin dress, combed her hair, and prepared to eat her first meal in her own "palace."

She stood smiling into the mirror. She did not know what lay ahead, but she was at home at last!

EIGHT

THE SCHOOL
IN THE PALACE

The next morning during breakfast a messenger appeared with an order from the King. Mrs. Leonowens was to present herself at court immediately. This was Thursday, the day of the week sacred to the god of wisdom, and therefore suitable for the opening of the school in the Grand Palace.

"Well!" said Anna, caught between surprise and annoyance. "I might have been told in advance!" She hurried to get ready, and soon she and Louis were in a long, narrow boat traveling to the Palace.

At the ornate river landing the messenger turned Anna and Louis over to slave girls, who led them to the pavilion that was to be used as the new school.

The approach to the pavilion was through a grove of orange and palm trees so thick that Anna and Louis moved in sun-flecked twilight. The slave girls signaled them to wait outside what seemed to be a temple and went in to announce their arrival. Anna stood among the tall golden pillars that reached up to the roof until one of the slaves beckoned. Then she took Louis by the hand and moved on into the temple itself, not knowing what to expect.

A colossal golden image of the Buddha dominated the great chamber. In the center of the floor stood a long table, finely carved, and some carved and gilded chairs. The King and most of the noble ladies of the court were present, with a few priests.

The King received Anna and Louis very kindly, with no hint of his previous ill temper. He pointed at two seats that had been prepared for them, then clapped his hands lightly, and the lower part of the hall filled with female slaves. A word or two from the King and the slaves withdrew. When they returned, crawling expertly across the floor on their knees and elbows, they were carrying slates, pencils, ink, pens, and English spelling books, which they placed on the table. Other women entered, also creeping, with burning tapers and vases full of white lotus flowers, which they set on the table in front of each of the twenty or more gilded chairs.

Then the priests chanted prayers. Anna looked around her. On one side and in front of the Buddha was an altar with offerings of small golden images set upon its various levels. Beyond this was a tall gilded chair where the chief of the priests sat. A few feet from the chair was the trunk of an old bo tree, carved with an image of the Indian god of wisdom.

When the chant ended, there was a ruffle of music from an unseen orchestra. This announced the entrance of the princes and princesses who were to be Anna's pupils. They advanced in the order of their age. First in line was a girl of about ten. Anna was struck by the rich satin of her skin, the delicacy of her form, and the luster of her dreamy eyes. The King took the girl gently by the hand and presented her to Anna, saying simply, "The English schoolmistress. Princess Ying Yaowalak, the first-born among women." The child's greeting was quiet and self-possessed. Taking both of Anna's hands between her own small ones, she bowed, touching them to her forehead. Then at a word from the King she retired to her place on the right. One by one all the royal children were presented. As the last child inched away along the floor to his place in the kneeling line, the music ceased.

The King then spoke briefly to his children, translating for Anna as he did so. "Dear children," he said, "it is our pleasure that you shall be educated in English as well as in your own language. Now as this is an English school, you will have to learn the English modes of etiquette and conversation. Each and every one of you shall be at liberty to sit in my presence in your chairs when I come to inspect the school. Unless, of course, it is your pleasure not to do so. In this I do not command you, but to study hard and make the best of your opportunities I do command you. This is a privilege no royal children have had before, and you are to make best use of it." The children all bowed, touching their foreheads to their folded palms on the floor.

This ended the ceremony, and the King departed with the priests. As Anna was beginning to wonder whether she should try to organize her school, slaves arrived and bore the royal children off—not only the youngest, but the bigger boys and girls of eight, nine, and ten. They were carried away in the arms of the women slaves as if they had been babies.

"Well!" thought Anna. Here was more evidence of how revolting slavery was, bad for the women who were slaves and bad for the children who were allowed to use other human beings to carry them as if they were animals.

Anna realized that school was over for the day, and that the ceremony had been merely the formal opening. "The King will send his messenger for me when he wants me again," she thought with a shrug, and set off to finish moving from the Kralahome's palace to her own new home.

A week later to the day, the serious business of the school began. Several old women, who had evidently been posted near the door to await Anna's arrival, flew off in various directions when she appeared. About an hour later they returned with twenty-one of the King's children. Anna was given a list of their names written in the King's own hand. The youngest was only five, the oldest ten. It was not long before they were ranged around the long table with a spelling book before each one, open at the first page. Anna placed Louis at the foot of the table while she went to the head.

The lesson began. Anna said the letters of the alphabet and the children recited them after her. Louis, his face serious with responsibility, had mounted a chair, the better to command his division. Out of the corner of her eye Anna could see him pointing with his small finger to one letter after the other as his class looked on, letters that were strange to them and, if truth were told, not perfectly familiar to him either.

At noon a number of young women were brought to Anna to be taught like the children, but no list of their names was provided. She received them with smiles and began to note their names in her book as they repeated them to her. But before she could begin the lesson, they began to study Anna intently, fingering her hair and pulling at her hairpins to examine them. One woman tried to put a hairpin in her own locks. It dropped out and they all laughed, for her hair was cut in a short brush not more than three inches long, as was the hair of all the women. They felt Anna's dress, particularly the belt and collar, and then her rings. Two of them lay flat on their stomachs, trying to peek under her skirt.

"For goodness sake! What is the matter?" she asked. "What do you want to know about my feet?" One woman who could speak Malay explained that the Palace had been seething with excited discussion of her figure ever since her first visit. The bell shape of her hoop skirts had convinced some of the women that she had a body that grew larger and larger downward and ended in feet big enough to fill the vast circle of her skirt.

"Mercy!" Anna exclaimed with a laugh, and lifted her hoops far enough for them to see that her feet and legs were like theirs, except for the shoes and stockings she wore.

"Ah-ah-ah!" they all breathed, entranced by this new knowledge.

Then a slave crouched down in front of Anna and pointed at the Englishwoman's nose. She wanted to ask, it seemed, whether Anna's nose had grown long from pulling, and also whether it had to be pulled every morning to keep it so. Anna assured her that the size of the nose was not a matter of exercise or choice on the part of its owner, but a work of nature. The slave clucked in sympathy and turned away fingering her own flatter nose with obvious preference.

The lesson was resumed.

Before long a few of the women drifted away, already bored with the effort of learning. But at the far end of the table, one was studying with rapt attention. She was a pale young woman. She bent over a little prince, apparently her son, with her eyes on the letters that Louis was naming to her. She alone of the whole group had paid no attention to the noise around her. Instead she had kept her eyes on her book, repeating to herself the strange names of the letters, as if the merriment of the others meant nothing to her. Now she stood apart and alone, concentrating on mastering the alphabet. When the hour for dismissal came, she repeated the entire lesson to Louis, who sat listening gravely. She finished the lesson correctly and Louis told her that she was "a very good child indeed," and that she might go.

She flushed with pleasure, but when she saw Anna watching her with curiosity, she crouched almost under the table, as if she had no right to be there. Anna saw that she was not so young as she had appeared at first. Her expressive eyes, full of sadness, looked at Anna now in alarm.

Anna decided to appear unconscious of the woman's presence and so encourage her to come again. She put on her bonnet, veil and gloves, and took Louis's hand. They walked out past the crouching woman and left the Palace quickly.

Anna guessed that the young woman had some-how displeased the King. In the universe of the harem with its thousands of moons circling the single great sun of the King, his disfavor was a terrible calamity; it made life hardly worth living. All the way home Anna thought about the woman. She had been a wife of the King and was the mother of one of his sons. Now she was an outcast for some reason or other. Perhaps she would welcome the world of knowledge that Anna had to offer.

Anna hoped so.

NINE

THE RED SNAKE

Anna's school was quickly organized. Classes began immediately after the nine o'clock service of worship in the temple, when the priests had withdrawn, and the ladies of the harem retired.

Mornings were devoted entirely to the royal children, some of whom showed the promise of being good scholars. In the afternoons any of the women who were interested were encouraged by the King to be present at the classes. The pale young woman whom

Anna had noticed on the first day came every afternoon and squatted behind her son or leaned over his shoulder, studying with an interest that would have set her apart, if her unhappy face had not done so already.

It was some time before Anna won the woman's confidence enough to ask her name. It was Son Klin, which meant "Hidden Perfume." Anna was too wise to single her out for special help or attention at first. She knew that any extra time spent with Son Klin would be noted instantly by the jealous eyes of the harem, and added somehow to the load of sorrow she already carried. Son Klin needed no special help, however. Her keen mind carried her along as rapidly as the best pupil in the class.

The Palace, and especially the harem, which was called the Inside, was a world in itself. When Anna and Louis entered the tall double gates each morning, they left the ordinary world behind and stepped into a glittering kingdom out of *The Arabian Nights*. At first Anna was too busy for anything but her schoolwork. When she had time she began to look around. The first places that she explored were the three Palace temples. The one in which Anna taught was called the Temple of the Mothers of the Free.

The general effect of these buildings was as awe-inspiring as any great European cathedral. Each was two hundred feet square with double rows of windows all around. The windows were flanked by pilasters and crowned with spiral canopies. The temple roofs rose in steeples, and these in turn were crowned by spires of gold rising more than a hundred and fifty feet from the ground.

The interiors were lined with large niches holding images of the Buddha. Some figures were standing, some sitting, and some were in the attitude of preaching showing him on a high, lotus-shaped pulpit made of the great snake, the Naga, whose cobra head formed an imposing sunshade. The vaulted cell in the main chamber of each temple, where the largest figure was seated, reached to the second or third level of the roof. A marvelous flood of sunlight streamed down from a small window in the roof itself.

Anna was told that according to tradition the temples had stood there for more than a thousand years. She came to know every inch of them, yet she was never able to understand fully their meaning and power. Whenever she passed along the dim and silent corridors, and came upon one of the great golden images amid the gloom—the head and shoulders illuminated by a halo from the unseen window above—she was compelled to stop. The Buddha, motionless with folded arms and drooping eyelids, looked down on her with the wisdom of ages stamped upon his brow.

Among her pupils, Anna's favorites were Prince Chulalongkorn, who was the heir apparent, and his pretty little sister, whom everyone called the Fa-ying, the Celestial Princess. They were both exceptionally bright children. Their young mother, the queen, had died the year before. They and their two younger brothers were living with an old great-aunt, a princess who lived in one of the most imposing palaces in the harem.

The old princess was a tranquil woman, attracted by everything that was bright and pretty. She was always busy with her flowers, or some poetry, or with the children. The little Fa-ying was her favorite, and after her, the young heir apparent. Her establishment was large, full of the daughters of her brothers, her nieces and nephews and friends. She was not only a very great lady, in whose house it was considered an honor to have a daughter living, but she was also famous for her goodness and kindness.

Anna and she had many conversations about the education of Prince Chulalongkorn. The old princess astonished Anna from the first by imploring her to instill into the mind of the young Prince the ideals and moral principles of Christianity. The princess saw no difference between her own religion and Anna's. What she wanted was to have her young charge fortified with all available goodness against what she knew lay in wait for a king.

Little Fa-ying was a fairy child. She was not only her great-aunt's favorite, but also her father's. Of all his sixty-seven children she was the one he loved the most. From the time she was a baby, the King had liked to have her near him. He held her on his lap at meals and even took her on royal tours as far away as Ayuthia.

Prince Chulalongkorn, too, was attractive. He was a good student, serene and gentle as well-bred Siamese boys were expected to be. He was affectionate to his old aunt and his younger sisters and brothers. And he had a warm heart that was aroused to sympathy by the mere sight of poverty or pain. In school he studied hard. Each new idea was like a discovery to him. It sometimes seemed to Anna that the Prince was hardly a child at all. The weight of the throne was already on him, and he knew his future would be full of heavy responsibilities. As Anna taught him from day to day, she doubled her efforts to help him in his eager search for knowledge. Who could say how soon vast and limitless power over the lives of millions of his subjects would be his?

The studies that interested the royal children most were geography and astronomy. Each of them had his own ideas about the form of the earth, and none of them believed that it was round. It took much patient repetition to convince them that it was neither flat nor square.

The only map they had ever seen was an old one that had been made perhaps twenty-five years before. It was five feet long and three wide, and it was not really a map at all. In the center was a field of red, twenty by twelve inches. This was Siam. A human figure as long as the red patch was cut out of silver paper and pasted on it. This was the King of Siam. On his head had been placed an enormous crown with many points, indicating his vast possessions. In one hand he held a breadfruit, symbol of plenty, and in the other what looked like a pitchfork, with which he sent destruction to all who opposed him.

On three sides of the map and a part of the fourth was a broad margin of blue, representing the ocean. Over it miniature ships, boats, and junks sailed in every direction to and from the land, showing the great amount of Siam's trade. Just above the patch of red was a smaller one of green, twelve by four inches, intended to represent Burma. In the center of this was drawn a rude figure without clothes or crown, the King of Burma. His lack of equipment showed how poor his kingdom was. Around him other rude figures, demons and goblins, danced. This was evidence of the disorder and misrule in his little realm. On the north side of the green patch was painted a large Englishman, wearing a cocked hat with red feathers—British Burma.

However little the children knew about the real world, they knew a great deal about a mythological world that Anna had never heard of. They loved to tell her about the mountains and seas and monsters of this never-never land. One of their favorite stories was about the giant turtle on whose back it all rested, and another about the immense fish that had churned the ocean when the world was forming.

Anna did not argue with them. Instead she sent a request to the King for maps and globes so that they could see for themselves. These created an enormous sensation when they arrived one morning in the Temple of the Mothers of the Free. The King had caused a large English map to be mounted in a heavy gold frame. He commanded that it be placed with the globes on gilt supporters in the middle of the temple. For nine days, crowds of women and children came to be taught geography and astronomy. They accepted the facts unquestioningly when they saw the map and globes, but it was hard for them to see Siam reduced to a mere speck on the great globe. Their only consolation was that England, the teacher's country, was smaller yet.

One day, as they were tracing the course of the river Nile, something happened that profoundly changed Anna's position in the harem. She had been courteously treated, but with a reserve that let her know she was an outsider, and not a very important one at that.

She was telling the children about her own long-ago trip through Egypt, when something suddenly fell from the vaulted roof above her head onto the table. It was a coil that looked like a thick silk cord neatly rolled into a ball.

In another instant the coil unrolled itself and began to move slowly away. Anna screamed, and forgetting her dignity, fled to the far end of the temple, expecting the children to follow her. When she turned she was amazed to see all her royal pupils sitting quietly in their seats, hands pressed together as if in prayer. Not a child had moved or made a sound. The temple was still. All the children's eyes were fixed on the serpent as it moved in lazy curves along the entire length of the table. With a feeling of shame, Anna returned to her seat to watch it. She even managed to share a little of the children's fascination as she looked into the clear eyes of the snake. She had never seen one like it. The upper part of it was a violet color. The sides were covered with scales of crimson edged with black. Beneath, it was a pale rose, and the tail ended in tints of bluish ash.

The snake moved on its slow way down the table. To Anna each second seemed an hour. She held her breath in terror as it dropped from the table to Prince Chulalongkorn's chair. What if the child moved and the snake struck? She had no doubt that her own life would be forfeited in a moment if the young Prince were to die under her care. She wanted to call out to him to hold perfectly still, but no sound came.

She did not need to worry, however, for he sat as motionless as the Buddha gleaming in the twilight behind him. Anna could not swallow or breathe until she saw the serpent glide from the chair and trail through the corridor and down the steps, and finally out of sight under the stone basement. Then she almost fainted from relief.

Not a child had stirred, and not a hand had been lowered from the position of salaam. But on the moment of the snake's disappearance the royal children jumped from their seats and clustered around her in the wildest joy. They fell at her feet. They salaamed her and caressed her, and chattered at her so fast that she could not grasp a word. As the news spread, the women of the harem came hurrying in to greet her affectionately and to salaam her as they had never done before. It was with the greatest difficulty that she finally learned what it was all about. They were trying to tell her that the gods evidently loved her, else they would not have sent such an auspicious token in favor of her teaching. They assured her that the gliding of the snake all over the table was full of happy omens, and that its dropping onto the arm of the Prince's chair was an unmistakable sign that he would one day become famous in wisdom and knowledge.

Nor was it an ordinary snake. This was the red snake that brought secret messages from the gods. The Siamese called it the *Ngu Thong Daeng*, the crimson-bellied snake, which brings to those who see it all that is good and great.

Anna hardly knew whether to be amused or annoyed or pleased. Even the King, when he heard of the behavior of the visitor, was impressed. He made the event known to the wise men of the court. They all united in pronouncing it a wonderful and inspiring recognition of favor from on high. Anna herself felt very uncomfortable for days after the sudden appearance of the snake. She secretly hoped that she would never be so favored by the gods again. But she did not mention her thoughts to the women of the harem. They, both young and old, continued to come and congratulate her during the week that followed, grasping her hands between theirs and raising them to their foreheads in admiration.

From that time on, Anna was treated with great respect.

TEN

INSIDE

The Grand Palace was not really a building at all, but a walled, fortified city that covered more than a square mile. Parallel walls running east and west divided it into three sections. The northern section was the seat of government. Here men came and went freely on official business.

The middle section was semiprivate; men were admitted only for certain work and on certain occasions. In it were the mint, which made the money for the kingdom, the King's printing press, and a number of pavilions, theaters, and aviaries, all richly gilded and ornamented. It was dominated by two buildings. One of them

was the Audience Hall of Indra, where Anna had first gone with Captain Bush. The other was the majestic temple of the Dusit Maha Prasat, where kings had been crowned and where their remains were kept in golden urns on the high golden altar.

The southern and third section was the most closely guarded of all. It was here that the King lived, here where the harem was situated, and here where Anna worked. This section, known as the Inside, was barred to all men but the King and his priests.

As Anna came to discover, it was an extraordinary place, a city in itself.

In back of the King's private quarters was a beautiful garden with a small artificial lake where the ladies of the harem came to bathe morning and evening. They spent many hours there on hot days, splashing about and picking water lilies.

Not far from the garden were the barracks of the Amazons and the pillared hall where female magistrates administered justice to the inhabitants of this city of women. Nearby, set in a grove, was the Temple of the Mothers of the Free, where Anna taught, and next to it the theater and gymnasium where the more important women assembled every afternoon to gossip, play games, and watch the dancing girls.

It did not take Anna long to discover that here, as in any other city, there were good residential areas and poor. Nearest the wall which divided the Inside from the center enclosure were some of the finest residences. Here were the palaces of the princesses, daughters of former kings, who were never allowed to marry unless the reigning king desired them. They were by law too high in rank to marry anyone else, and a foreign alliance was unthinkable. Here also lived the more favored of the royal wives with their children, their numerous slaves, and their personal ladies-in-waiting and maids. There were clean, regular streets and small parks, groups of fine trees scattered over miniature lawns, and beautiful flower gardens.

In the southern part of the city, which was the most crowded, were markets, shops, and slave quarters.

Anna learned that, though slave women could go outside the walls to visit their husbands for months at a time, their mistresses almost never left the Inside. The King allowed his consorts and ladies-in-waiting to leave for important occasions—the cremation of parents, for example—but even then, the privilege had to be obtained from him in writing, and it was not always granted. If it were, large tips to the Amazon guards were also required. So for most of the women the harem was the world—a world of nine thousand women within the confines of its high walls.

The women themselves seemed an indistinguishable mass of human beings to Anna at first, but as time went on the mass broke up into people, many of whom she came to regard as her friends. She soon knew the mothers of her pupils through the children. Their position as Mothers of Royal Children set them apart (of the nine thousand women only about thirty were so honored). Most of these were the daughters of noblemen and had been offered for the royal service by their families. Some had lived in the Palace since childhood as maids-in-waiting to one or another of the princesses. Each princess had her own space, large or small, with many little maids, and each must make a life out of her narrow sphere.

Some did embroidery work, and taught their maids-in-waiting to do it also. Some made wax and paper flowers for cremations and for temple decorations. Others were skilled in weaving fragile chandeliers, table covers, and even curtains in lacy patterns of rose petals, jessamine, and other flowers, threaded in beautiful designs for important festivals. Some read novels, poetry, and plays and taught their small maids to read also. And some spent endless hours gambling.

The little maids did light tasks for their mistresses in return for education in the refinements of Palace life. There were no schools for girls anywhere in Siam, so it was only girls so trained who had any opportunity for an education. All the Palace arts were highly prized. They were the mark of the cultivated woman. It was considered an honor for a family to have a daughter in the Palace in this or any other capacity.

The royal consorts as well as the princesses had the daughters of relatives and friends entrusted to them. They, too, had their own establishments and possessed slaves. The allowances made to them by the King were hardly adequate for the simplest living, but many were independently wealthy. If they pleased the King, he gave them rich possessions in addition to their allowances so that they became immensely wealthy in two or three years, while others lived and died poor.

Some of the consorts and most of the princesses were very haughty, and insisted on every ounce of honor their positions entitled them to. Many, however, were gracious and charming. One of these, who became Anna's fast friend, was Lady Thiang, mother of Anna's pupil Princess Somawadi. She was a woman of about thirty, with jet black hair and eyes. She was clever and kind, although compared to some of the more intelligent women of the harem, she was not highly educated.

But she was the mother of more of His Majesty's children than any other woman, even though she had never been his favorite wife at any time. She had borne four daughters and three sons to the King. Now that both queens were dead she had become head wife by common consent and by the admiration in which she was held. Of all the women in the Palace she alone, it seemed to Anna, really loved the King. She managed to always be in his favor, serving him with gentleness and understanding. He in turn recognized her trustworthiness by raising her to the important position of superintendent of the royal kitchens. This position carried with it many privileges, among them two houses. One was her home, where her children were born and brought up. The other was next door to the royal kitchens, and there she spent most of each day selecting and sometimes preparing dishes for the royal table.

Her natural friendliness had made her generally loved, and her immense wealth and influence seemed only to have broadened her sympathies. She was always ready to help the other women of the harem when they were in trouble, even when she had to hide what she was doing from the King. She reconciled her little deceptions by saying: "Surely it is better for *HIM* not to know everything. *HE* knows too much already with *HIS* Siamese and English and Pali and Sanskrit. I wonder *HE* can ever get to sleep at all with so many different tongues in *HIS* head."

The executive staff of the harem was very large and included four hundred Amazon guards, twelve judges, stewards (whose duty it was to take care of the royal possessions), undertakers, and many other officers, all women. The most interesting to Anna was the chief of the judges of the women's court. Like most of the executive officers, she was not and never had been a royal consort. Her title was Khun Thao Ap, and she was an unusually tall and commanding woman, and very dark, with soft eyes in a heavy face. In spite of her enormous power, the judge's way of life was simple. She lived alone in a small house at the end of one of the main streets, where she could easily be reached. She had freed her slaves, and was attended by four loyal servants.

Khun Thao Ap and Anna soon became friends, sharing a wry sense of humor and a love of learning. Though they never spoke of it, Anna sensed that she and the judge also shared a deep hatred of slavery. Much later—and in a very dramatic fashion—she learned that this was true.

ELEVEN

THE KING
AND THE FA-YING

The world within the Palace walls was a universe with a single sun and many moons. The King was the disk of light around which everything revolved. What he did day by day determined what the women of the harem did. Even the English school

had to be adjusted to the orbit of the King's life. He rose at five. So, therefore, did most of the members of the household. After a scanty meal, he descended to the courtyard and took his place on a strip of matting, laid from one gate of the Inside through all the avenues to another. His children were seated on his right in the order of their rank, then the princesses, his maids of honor, and their slaves. Before each person was placed a large silver tray containing offerings of boiled rice, fruit, cakes, and siri leaf, which some of the women had arisen hours earlier to prepare. There were occasionally cigars.

A little after five the gate called the Gate of Merit was thrown open and a hundred and ninety-nine priests entered. As the priests came toward the royal family they chanted, "Take thy meat, but think it dust! Eat but to live, and but to know thyself, and what thou art below! And say unto thy heart, 'It is the earth I eat, that to the earth I may new life impart.'"

The chief priest led the procession. He advanced with downcast eyes and presented his bowl, which hung from his neck by a cord. If anyone before whom a bowl was placed was not ready, no priest stopped. All continued to advance slowly, taking what was offered without thanks or even a look of acknowledgment until the end of the long row had been reached. Then the procession retired, chanting as before.

After this the King withdrew to his private temple, where he spent an hour in prayer and meditation.

This service over, he retired for a nap, and when he awoke, his breakfast was served with intricate formality. After he had inspected the gifts on the pavement before the Palace, he entered an antechamber of the women's Audience Hall where a large number of the harem ladies waited. He seated himself at a long table, frequently with little Fa-ying on his lap. Twelve women knelt nearby before great silver trays filled with twelve varieties of food—soups, meats, game, poultry, fish, vegetables, cakes, jellies, preserves, sauces, fruits, and teas. Each tray in its order was passed by three ladies to the head wife, Lady Thiang, who removed the silver cover, and at least seemed to taste the contents of the dish. Then, advancing on her knees, she set the dishes one by one on the table before the King.

Actually the King ate very little of the lavish food, although he often spent much time urging it on the princess. He ate sparingly and healthily. It was amusing to watch him solemnly eating with gold chopsticks only a modest bowl of boiled rice.

At these leisurely breakfasts it was his custom to talk with Anna, and it was at this hour that she came to know the King well, to admire and respect his brilliant mind. She believed him to be the most systematically educated, the most eager devourer of books and news, of any crowned head of the day. He passed the rest of the morning in study or correspondence. Anna was usually free to carry on her school during this time. If the King was tired, he took another nap at noon. If not, he continued to study until two o'clock, when he put aside his books and letters and sent a golden candlestick to the Temple of the Emerald Buddha.

As Anna had seen on her first visit to the Palace, this was the signal that the King had begun to prepare for his public appearance. Immediately all the narrow, crooked streets and lanes which intersected and crossed each other in such bewildering irregularity were thronged with women and children of every age. This stream of humanity, some in silks and some in rags, moved rapidly and wordlessly toward the Audience Hall of women.

Those of lesser rank knelt on the pavement outside, while around the hall itself, hundreds of princesses and ladies-in-waiting knelt to await the King's appearance. In the meantime the King descended to the dining salon, where he was served the most substantial meal of the day, then entered the Audience Hall and chatted with his favorites among the wives and children. The love of children was his one constant virtue.

When the King had dismissed the women and

children, he would go to the outside Hall of Audience to consider official matters with the members of his government. Twice a week at sunset he appeared at one of the gates of the Palace to hear the petitions of the common people, who were sometimes too over-whelmed by the glory of his presence to submit the precious petitions they had brought.

At nine he retired for the night. Around twelve or one he woke from his first sleep, and devoted several hours to study or letter writing. If he found a word in his reading that he could not understand, he would send a dozen or more slave women for Anna. Usually these words were technical or scientific terms not found in the dictionary, and not in Anna's head, either. Her inability to define them never failed to anger the King. He would look at her indignantly and say, "Why for you do not know? It's clear that you aren't scientific!"

Twice a week at midnight the King held a secret council of the San Luang (the Royal Inquisition). Anna never obtained any clear knowledge of the dark and terrifying proceedings of this secret court, for she never attended a session, nor would anyone talk about it with her. Certain things she learned, however, as time passed. The San Luang was silent and secretive. It proceeded without witnesses or warning, kidnapping and then imprisoning suspects until they confessed.

The San Luang was so feared that no man would consent to appear before it even as a witness except for a large reward. The wise citizen was careful to find a protector in some formidable friend who was a member. Spies in the employ of the San Luang penetrated every family of wealth and influence.

On several occasions when Anna was more than usually annoyed by the King, she gave vent to her feelings in word or look. She soon observed that if this happened in the presence of certain officers and courtiers they rapped in a peculiar, stealthy manner. This tapping, she discovered, was one of the secret signs of the San Luang. The warning signal was addressed to her because they imagined that she was also a member of the San Luang staff, since her influence with the King had grown so great. When she found this out, she knew that she had ceased to be merely a pawn on the chessboard of Palace life. She had become a player in the game.

The work of the school itself progressed rapidly, and this delighted the King. Prince Chulalongkorn continued to be outstanding among the children. He was methodical in his work and very serious about it. He moved ahead with a steady, even progress that was gratifying to his teacher and doubly so to his father. He was more self-disciplined than the rest of the children, and often helped keep his small brothers and sisters under control.

His little sister, the Fa-ying, besides being the favorite of her father, was an exceptionally beautiful child. She had soft, dark eyes filled with a trustfulness that was very winning. The late queen had entrusted her three sons and her daughter to their royal father with tenderness and anxiety shortly before her own death. The King had been deeply moved by her concern for them. As he loved the mother, so now he loved the children, and the Fa-ying more than the others. In a fumbling way he lavished on her a love intended to take the place of her mother's. When she was hardly more than a baby he had assigned to her the best of the tutors among the women of the harem.

The Fa-ying loved the English school and especially the pictures in her English books. She grew very fond of pictures of the Christ Child. Whenever she was tired of studying, she would jump up into Anna's lap and settling down comfortably, say, "Tell me a story! Tell me all about your beautiful Jesus!"

After Anna had told her a story, the Fa-ying would smile and pat Anna's cheeks and say, "I, too, little Fa-ying, I love your sacred Jesus very much. Do He love me a little, very little? I no got mother, poor little Fa-ying! Could He love her too?"

Consciously Anna tried to shape the little princess

to a pattern of kindness. The child received whatever she asked for from her father, and it was Anna's hope that some day the Fa-ying would choose to make life in the harem better for the thousands of women that must live there. Like her brother, Prince Chulalongkorn, she had an innate sympathy for those who suffered.

One afternoon as Anna worked alone, she was interrupted by a small, bell-like voice. "Will you teach me to draw, Mem *cha*? I want to make some pretty pictures." It was the Fa-ying.

"I like my English teacher and I like English. There are so many pretty pictures in my English books. And I want to draw some myself. So will you teach me to draw, Mem *cha*?" The Fa-ying climbed into Anna's lap and curled up like a kitten. Anna put down her pen to make room. Although the princess was almost eight years old, she was no larger than a four-year-old English child.

"I'll be glad to teach you to draw, if your father doesn't object," Anna promised. The Fa-ying slipped her arms around the Englishwoman's neck and gave her a delighted hug that reminded Anna of her own daughter. "Let's go and ask His Majesty if you may study drawing, shall we?" she asked.

The Fa-ying sprang to the floor and seized Anna's

hand. "Oh, yes, let's go right now!" So they went and put their request before the King in his upstairs study. His face softened as he looked at the little girl. And he smiled at Anna, pleased by her interest in his favorite child. He made no objection to his daughter's request, and day after day she came to Anna in the late afternoon while the other children had lessons with their Sanskrit tutors. It was a pleasant interlude in the regular routine of Anna's busy life.

Sometimes the little girl would draw or paint. Sometimes she would sit quietly and watch Anna draw. If she grew tired, she climbed into Anna's lap and demanded a Bible story. She had her favorites, which she insisted on hearing over and over. Anna marveled at the spiritual understanding of her alert small mind and at her ability to grasp the meaning of the stories. If the little princess and her brother, given all the power that was theirs by birth and position, fulfilled their promise, the Siam of the next generation would be a better place than the Siam of 1863.

TWELVE

ELEPHANTS

Pleased as the King was with the progress of his children, it never seemed to occur to him that it would have been even quicker if he had not summoned Anna from her schoolroom every time he wanted an English letter written.

King Mongkut demanded Anna's assistance with his English and French letters. His Majesty's correspondence was enormous. During years of meditation and study his mind had been probing the scientific

knowledge of the West, especially astronomy. This interest was the source of many exchanges of letters with men of science all over the world. But the bulk of his correspondence had been undertaken for diplomatic reasons, and the most important part of it was with Queen Victoria. The King used to begin his letters to her with elaborate formality:

> *Somdetch Phra Paramendr Maha Mongkut,*
> *by the Divine blessing of the Superagency of the*
> *Universe the First King of the Siamese kingdom,*
> *consisting of Siamese proper both Northern and*
> *Southern and the adjacent tributary dependencies,*
> *Laos, Cambodia and several provinces of Malay*
> *peninsula*
>   *&c*   *&c*   *&c*
> *To her Gracious Majesty Victoria the Queen of*
> *the United Kingdom of Great Britain and Ireland,*
> *the powerful Sovereign of British Colonies almost*
> *around the Globe of Human world,*
>   *&c*   *&c*   *&c*
> *Our most respected and distinguished Friend,*
> *and by race of the royalty our very affectionate*
> *Sister.*
> *Humble and respectfully sendeth Greetings.*

Queen Victoria replied not only with letters but with gifts. Part of the King's expression of appreciation reads as follows:

> *We on this occasion have liberty to let our native photographers take the likeness of ourselves, when we adorned with the watch decked with diamonds and the double edged sword, which were honorary royal gracious gift from your Majesty, received by us a few years ago, and seated ourselves by the tables containing the gift silver inkstand and desk together with the revolving pistol and rifle, wholly being royal gracious gift from your Majesty.*

Nor was the King to be outdone in the sumptuousness of his gifts to the Queen. According to his own list these included

I. The Royal official customary letter slightly written in Siamese characters upon a solid golden plate and wrapped in the Royal solid golden envelope and sealed with Royal peculiar seal and enclosed in a golden case richly enamelled.

The translation of this Royal letter in English annexed or appended herewith.

This is made according to the Siamese Royal custom for very respectful compliment to the Sovereign of Superior Kingdom, not to the equal or inferior always—when the superior Sovereign does not allow to be omitted.

2. Two Royal Daguerreotype portraits, one of which is a likeness of His Majesty the First King of Siam dressed in full royal robes and decorations seated on his throne of state.

The other is the Daguerreotype of His Majesty with the Royal consort and two Royal children seated in Their Majesties knees.

3. A Royal Crown beautifully enamelled and set with diamonds.

4. A Royal Ribbon with circular gold brooches richly set with rubies locked together and fixed all round with blue satin.

And so on through thirty-four elaborate and costly gifts, and sixty-four samples of merchandise mentioned in a tariff schedule that the King had negotiated with the British.

This correspondence was, of course, no random affair. It was shrewdly calculated to further friendly relations between Siam and England. The King had seen the growing British kingdom add several nearby countries to its empire, despite the efforts of their rulers against it. He was convinced that the best way to protect his own country was through a friendship with the Queen. If any of her officers attacked him or threatened to attack, he planned to appeal directly to her, relying on the friendship that he had carefully fostered through the years.

Before Anna came to Siam he had also begun a correspondence with President Abraham Lincoln of the United States. The King had read that in the traveling circuses which were very popular in the rural areas of the United States, the elephant was regarded as the most remarkable and interesting of the animals on display. Siam was the home of the elephant. Thousands roamed its jungles, and they were all the property of the King. The King immediately thought of a service that he might render the United States. He wrote:

> *Somdetch Phra Paramendr Maha Mongkut, by the blessing of the highest superagency of the whole universe, the King of Siam, the sovereign of all interior tributary countries adjacent and around in every direction, viz: Laws of Shiengs on northwestern and northern; Law Kaus on northern to northeastern to southeastern; most of the Malay peninsula on southern and southwestern; and Kariengs on the western to northwestern points, and the*

professor of the Magadhe language and Budhistical literature, &c., &c., &c., to his most respected excellent presidency, the President of the United States of America, who, having been chosen by the citizens of the United States as most distinguished, was made President and Chief Magistrate in the affairs of the nation for an appointed time of office.

It has occurred to us that if, on the continent of America, there should be several pairs of young male elephants turned loose in forest where there was abundance of water and grass, in any region under the sun's declination both north and south, called by the English the torrid zone, and all were forbidden to molest them, to attempt to raise them would be well, and if the climate there should prove favorable to elephants, we are of the opinion that after a while they will increase until they become large herds, as there are here on the continent of Asia, until the inhabitants of America will be able to catch and tame and use them as beasts of burthen, making them of benefit to the country, since elephants, being animals of great size and strength, can bear burdens and travel through uncleared woods and matted jungles, where no carriage and cart roads have yet been made.

We on our part, will procure young male and

female elephants, and forward them, one or two pairs at a time.

When the elephants are on board the ship, let a steamer take it in tow, that it may reach America as rapidly as possible, before they become wasted and diseased by the voyage.

When they arrive in America do not let them be taken to a cold climate out of the regions under the sun's declinations or torrid zone, but let them with all haste be turned out to run wild in some jungle suitable for them, not confining them any length of time.

If these means can be done, we trust that the elephants will propagate their species hereafter in the continent of America.

Mr. Lincoln already had a great deal on his hands with the Civil War, but his reply was courteous:

I appreciate most highly your Majesty's tender of good offices in forwarding to this government a stock from which a supply of elephants might be raised on our own soil. This government would not hesitate to avail itself of so generous an offer if the object were one which could be made practically useful in the present condition of the United States.

Our political jurisdiction, however, does not reach a latitude so low as to favor the multiplication of the elephant, and steam on land, as well as on water, has been our best and most efficient agent of transportation in internal commerce.

I shall have occasion at no distant day to transmit to your Majesty some token or indication of the high sense which this government entertains of your Majesty's friendship.

Meantime, wishing for your Majesty a long and happy life, and for the generous and emulous people of Siam the highest possible prosperity, I commend both to the blessings of Almighty God.

Your good friend,
Abraham Lincoln.
Washington, February 3, 1862.
By the President: William H. Seward, Secretary of State.

Anna was soon to see an even more striking demonstration of the King's love of elephants. One morning a group of her pupils came running into the pavilion crying, "Mem, Mem, he has come! The great prince has come! Isn't it wonderful?"

"What prince has come?" she asked, thinking it was strange that she had not heard of the visiting royalty in advance.

"The white elephant! The white elephant! Our guardian angel prince!" they shouted together. As the news spread over the city, royal and peasant, master and slave, young and old congratulated each other in jubilation. Prayers and offerings were made immediately in all the temples. The town crier who shouted the news along the streets was showered with gifts of money, cloth, rice, and bottles of perfumed oil.

Seventy-five royal barges and a hundred boats were prepared at once with a week's supplies to take the King and his family, the Amazons, and various court officers to the place where the white elephant had been found. Anna asked permission to go with the royal party to the old capital of Ayuthia. The animal had been sighted there during the annual roundup of elephants in the forest.

Before sunset the procession left, accompanied by the firing of guns and the shouts of thousands of people who lined the riverbanks. The boats reached Ayuthia the next morning. The court then transferred to horses and rode for miles through beautiful country to the kraal, or stockade, where the roundup was to take place. As soon as they arrived at the King's palace on the north side of the kraal, they climbed a steep flight of stairs to an open tower with a magnificent view of the countryside. The kraal itself lay before them, made of heavy piles driven into the ground very closely to form a circle three or four miles in diameter.

Beside the tower was a chamber that held an immense drum, around which twelve men waited to signal the beginning of the chase. A hundred and fifty trained elephants stood before the palace. There were two men on each, one at the back with a forked goad to urge the beast ahead, and one in the front armed with lances, spears, and a quiver of arrows. The moment the royal party appeared, the elephants wheeled and formed a semicircle. Each hunter raised his spear in salute. There was a shouted command and the great beasts sank to their knees and raised their trunks into the air, bringing them down in a mass salaam.

A moment later, the colossal drum thundered the signal for the hunt. The company of elephants divided and spread out through the countryside where the wild elephants were grazing. The royal party could see the hunting elephants appear and disappear through the trees for many miles. Round and round they went, each time decreasing the circle of their movements and hemming the wild beasts into a smaller and smaller compass. Sometimes they could be seen distinctly; sometimes they were lost for a while in the clumps of forest. Then came a terrific succession of wild trumpetings from the trapped elephants and shouts from the hunters, "Don't let them escape!" and a deafening peal of bugles, horns, and trumpets.

As the wild elephants moved nearer, the shouts grew shriller, until at last the court could see the animals plunging madly, caught in a perfect circle formed by the hunters on their mounts. All at once a tremendous black creature thought he saw an opening close by and made a break for it through the entrance to the kraal right into the hunters' trap. In charged the whole herd, screaming with anger and fright, their trunks thrown high in the air. It was almost noon and the hunt was successfully over. To the joy of the royal party one great salmon-colored beast—the "white" one—heaved and trumpeted in the sea of gray and black ones.

For hours the trapped animals ran back and forth, lashing the solid posts with their trunks, twisting them and trying to uproot them, throwing their weight against the barrier of piles. All in vain. The sun set and the weary beasts finally huddled close together with the white elephant in their midst.

The next morning they tried again to free themselves. It was afternoon before they became so faint from hunger that they gave up and tore branches from trees growing in the stockade to eat. This was a sign for the hunters on the tame elephants to enter the kraal. About sixty men with fine grass, cut and prepared, and heaps of sugar cane followed the hunters. The tame beasts were turned loose while the newly trapped elephants were tempted with the grass and cane. In a few moments they all flocked around the men and began to feed. In less than half an hour the wild elephants took what was given them without snatching and even fondled with their long trunks the hands of the men that fed them. Meanwhile, other men fastened chains to their legs and bound them to the tame elephants.

The white elephant alone was not bound to another of its kind. Several long silken cords were fastened about his neck and these were tied to one of the posts of the kraal. Immediately a wide path was cleared for him to the river where his journey to Bangkok would begin. A day or so later, when it was complete, a gold cloth was laid on his back and the party set out on their triumphant return to the capital. Even the King played second fiddle to the new "prince." In front of the elephant young girls danced and sang and played musical instruments; a number of men performed feats of strength and skill—tumbling, wrestling, and knocking each other down for the "prince's" amuse-ment. Other men fanned him and fed him. Priests prayed for him. When he reached the river he was placed on a floating palace of wood, covered by a gorgeous roof and hung with crimson curtains. This he seemed to dislike in spite of the fact that the roof was literally thatched with flowers, ingeniously arranged to form symbols and mottoes, which the beast was supposed to be able to read with ease.

The floor of the barge was covered with a gilt mat woven in curious patterns. The elephant was installed in the middle of this. Around him were stationed attendants who bathed and perfumed him, sang lullabies to him, fanned him and praised him all the way to the capital. The royal barges were carefully steered beside his float so that the King and nobles, using silken cords, could help to float him down the river.

News of the "prince's" imminent arrival had preceded him to Bangkok, and he was greeted with shouts of joy, the beating of drums, the sound of trumpets, and the boom of cannons. A great company was waiting to meet him on the riverbank and to follow him to the Palace. There the lordly beast was knighted, as a conch shell of holy water was poured over his head. The title by which he was ennobled was Phya Sri Wongsi Decha Saralai Krasat, which meant "Handsome Lord of Powerful Family." Gold rings were fastened around his tusks, a gold chain was hung around his neck, and a purple velvet cloak, fringed with scarlet and gold, was thrown over him.

For seven days the elephant was pampered and petted while the whole city engaged in a carnival to celebrate this token of favor from on high. Anna discovered that, contrary to what many foreigners believed, the Siamese did not worship the albino as a god. They did believe, however, that Buddha, in each successive reincarnation, occupied in turn the forms of white animals of certain classes, particularly the swan, the stork, the white sparrow, the dove, the monkey, and the elephant. They thought that the forms of these creatures were reserved for the souls of the good and great. Thus almost all white animals were held in reverence. The white elephant, in particular, was supposed to be inhabited by the spirit of some king or hero. Since he had once been a great man, he was thought to be familiar with the dangers that surround the great, and to know what was best for the nobles of the day. So the white elephant, therefore, was supposed to avert national calamity and bring prosperity and peace to the people.

The "prince" was fed the finest herbs, the tenderest grass, the sweetest sugar cane, the mellowest bananas, and the most delicious cakes, served on huge trays of gold and silver. His water was perfumed with jessamine. Sadly, it was all too much for him. He was taken with a severe attack of indigestion during the seventh night, and although the King's own doctor was summoned, he died in a few hours.

No man dared to carry the tidings to the King. But the Kralahome called up thousands of slaves and pulled down the new stables. They worked in nervous haste, terrified that the King might come before they were through. It was not until the cool of the late afternoon that he appeared, to see for himself the progress of the building. When his gaze met nothing but vacancy and a large patch of bare earth, the truth flashed upon him at once. The little Fa-ying, who had been coached for the part, knelt before him and said, "Weep not, O my father. Perhaps the stranger lord has left us but for a time." The King was grief-stricken.

The whole nation went immediately into mourning. Although the elephant was counted royal, he was not cremated. His carcass was shrouded in fine white linen and laid on a bier. It was then floated down the river with much wailing and many dirges to be deposited at last in the Gulf of Siam.

The King memorialized the white elephant in a proclamation issued by the royal press. He read it to Anna later when normal life had once more begun. Part of it described the dead animal: "His eyes were light blue, surrounded by a beautiful salmon color; his hair was fine, soft and long; his complexion pinkish white; his tusks like long white pearls; his ears like silver shields; his trunk like a comet's tail; his legs like the feet of the sky; his tread like the sound of thunder; his looks full of meditation; his expression full of tenderness; his cry like the voice of a mighty warrior; and his whole bearing like that of an illustrious monarch."

It reminded Anna of the description of Queen Victoria written by the King's ambassador on his return from her court some years before. He had said of her: "One cannot but be struck with the aspect of the august Queen of England, or fail to observe that she must be of pure descent from a race of goodly and warlike kings and rulers of the earth, in that her eyes, complexion, and above all her bearing, are those of a beautiful and majestic white elephant."

THIRTEEN

THE MANSION OF
THE BRASS DOOR

May 2, 1863, was a day that Anna would never forget. She had gone as usual to her temple schoolroom just as the great clock on the tower struck nine. Louis had not come with her that day because he had had a slight touch of fever. The Temple of the

Mothers of the Free was empty. Her pupils, she learned, were absent at a ceremony on the other side of the Palace, and word had been left that she was to attend. It was the Festival of the Birth, Enlightenment, and Death of the Buddha, one of the most important religious occasions of the year.

Anna set off at once. She was careful to attend every ceremony to which she was invited, for she was determined to understand the culture around her. Every time she thought that she *did* understand it, something would happen to show her that the Inside was as confusing and unknowable as ever. Most confusing of all was the knowledge that here was a jail where women and children innocent of any crime were imprisoned for life. She doubted she would ever understand or accept that fact.

On this particular morning the Inside seemed to have been emptied of its inhabitants. Anna had set off to find the temple where the ceremony was taking place, but she had no clear idea of which street to take. After some random wandering she met a flower girl who gave her directions. Following these, she entered a long dark alley, passed into another, and then another. The alleys soon brought her to a gloomy street. No sunlight penetrated between the blank house walls that lined it. The farther end was veiled in mist and darkness.

Anna walked on more slowly, convinced that she had lost her way. She looked first on one side and then on the other for a cross street, but there was none. Nor did she meet anyone along the entire length of it. There was something about the alley that gave her the uneasy feeling it was not intended for public use. Suddenly she reached the end, a high brick wall.

She paused and looked about. Behind her stretched the alley. Before her was a door of polished brass. The din of Palace life was not fifteen minutes away, and yet the solitude of the place was strangely hushed. Its soundlessness was eerie. As Anna stood there, listening to the unnatural silence, she felt goose flesh along her arms. "None of that!" she scolded herself, and, ashamed of her panic, she threw her weight against the heavy door and pushed.

With well-oiled ease it swung open—slowly, noiselessly. She stepped into a paved courtyard. There was a garden on the right, a building on the left. The wall ran all around and enclosed both. The walks of the garden were bordered with small Chinese trees planted in straight rows. Grass covered half of them and moss the rest. The facade of the mansion was decayed and gloomy—the windows were closed, and those on the upper story had heavy shutters like a prison.

A slight movement drew Anna's eyes away from the house. In the middle of the garden, near a small pond, a woman was sitting on the ground, nursing a child. She was large and strongly made, yet her features were gaunt, and long matted hair hung around her shoulders.

Anna had made up her mind to ask for help in finding the temple, but the moment she approached the woman and child she was overwhelmed by a choking surge of pity. The woman was chained to a post driven into the ground. Under her lay a tattered fragment of matting, and farther on were a block of wood for a pillow and several broken Chinese umbrellas. These, it seemed, were her only protection against the burning sky.

The woman made no sound, but kept her eyes on the white stranger. Anna sat down on the rim of the pool and looked at her helplessly. Once more she was confronted with the apathy and callousness of harem life. Even a dangerous criminal should not have been left unprotected beneath the merciless tropical sun. But here sat this slave, almost without clothes, her filthy hair in dense masses around her face. The mat, the pillow, the broken umbrellas, all testified to the fact that she had been there a long time. Unrelenting heat pulsed around her. Rain no doubt buffeted her. She had been degraded to a level where no amount of decency could be expected of her, yet here she was, caring for her child.

Indignant questions churned to the surface of Anna's mind. She could have wept from the anger that pounded in her breast. But she was silent for several minutes, unable to command her voice. At last she asked the woman her name.

"*Pai sia!*" (Go away!) was the savage reply.

Anna tried again. "Why are you chained here? Won't you tell me? You don't need to be afraid of me."

"*Pai! Pai! Pai!*" screamed the woman. The child set up a howling which echoed and re-echoed from the walls. The woman turned and took him in her arms, and he was quiet in an instant. He was a sturdy little fellow, covered with dirt but healthy. She rocked him back and forth, her face resting against his unwashed cheek.

A little puff of wind shook the hot blanket of air. A coconut loosened by the nibbling of a squirrel dropped with a loud clack in a far corner of the garden. Anna rose from the wall of the pond and sat down on the blistering pavement beside the woman and child. Very gently she asked the child's age.

The slave looked at her with mistrust. "He is four," she said curtly.

"And what is his name?"

"His name is Thuk" (Sorrow), the slave answered reluctantly, turning away her face.

"And why did you give him such a name?"

The woman looked at Anna and something blazed in her eyes, but it was gone in an instant. She relapsed into silence, gazing dully at the empty air, and the three of them sat that way for several minutes. Then Anna heard a strangled cry. With her face hidden behind her bare arms, the woman began to sob. At this her little boy wailed piercingly. The woman quieted him, and then turned to Anna.

"Were you sent to find me by my husband, lady?" she asked hoarsely. "Have you come to buy me? O, please buy me, lady, please! Help me to get my pardon!"

"Why are you chained here?" asked Anna. "Have you committed some crime?"

This seemed a terrible question. The woman's face twisted, but no sound came from them. Again she threw her arms over her head and wept. Her body rocked back and forth, racked with passionate sobbing, while Anna looked on alarmed and helpless. After a while she became quiet, and turning her face to Anna, said bitterly, "Do you want to know my crime? It was loving my husband."

Anna was more puzzled than ever. "But if that was

the case, why did you leave him and become a slave here in the Palace?"

"Gracious lady, I was born a slave. It was the will of Allah."

The use of the word "Allah" gave Anna a clue. "Are you a Mohammedan?" she asked.

"My parents were Mohammedans, slaves of the father of my mistress. When we were very young my brother and I were sent as slaves to her daughter in the Palace."

"If you can prove that your parents were Mohammedans, I think I may be able to help you. All the Mohammedans here are under British protection, and no subject of Britain can be made a slave."

"But, gracious lady, my parents sold themselves to my mistress's grandfather."

"That was their debt, which they have paid over and over again by their faithful service. You can insist that your mistress accept your purchase money."

"Insist!" the slave's eyes blazed. "Do you know who my mistress is? She is the daughter of the Minister of the North, the most powerful man in the kingdom next to the Kralahome! I insist?" She laughed bitterly. "She was one of the wives of the late King! The present Lord of Life is her son-in-law! Not only that, her daughter was his favorite for a long time, and is still high in his graces. *Insist?* I, who was born a slave?" The fire that had lighted the woman's eyes faded away. "No, I cannot insist that my mistress take my purchase money. My only chance for freedom is a pardon, and she will never give it to me."

"But what about your friends outside the Palace?" asked Anna. "Surely there's something they can do. Have you sent them word of your captivity?"

"No, I was taken too suddenly. I fear they think I am dead. I speak with nobody, not even to the slave who brings me my food. And her life is so hard that she cannot run the risk of carrying a message outside the Palace for me.

"My disappearance is still a mystery after four years. No one comes here but my mistress, and she only visits once in a while with the most trusted of her slaves. Now that she is old the King lets her go in and out of the Palace as she likes. Every few weeks some of her slaves come to trim the trees in the garden or clean the house, but they have nothing to do with me." There was despair in her voice. "There is no one to help me. I shall be chained here until I die. No one cares any more but my husband. And he doesn't know where I am."

The eleven o'clock bell boomed through the solitude. The woman lay down beside the sleeping boy to rest, apparently worn out by the emotional effort of talking. Anna placed her own small umbrella over the head of the slave in such a way as to shield her eyes and those of the boy. This simple act of kindness so touched the slave that she started up suddenly and, before Anna could prevent it, kissed Anna's shoes. Anna's eyes filled with tears.

"Little sister," she said, using the gentle Siamese term, "tell me your whole story from beginning to end and I'll lay it before the King."

The woman sat up swiftly and adjusted the umbrella over her sleeping child.

"My name, gracious lady, is L'Ore," she began, "and I was born a slave. My mistress the Chao Chom rewarded my faithful service by making me the first attendant to Princess Butri, an honor for which I was grateful. Then one day she handed me a large sum of money and sent me on an errand to buy Bombay silk.

"It was the first time I had been outside the Palace in years, and as our boat pushed onto the river, I began to feel as if I was in some intoxicating dream. Everything—the sunlight on the river, the trees, the cries of the birds, the flowers—filled me with delight."

Anna listened to L'Ore with fascination, wondering if the girl had been trained to sing or recite poetry, for she spoke with great eloquence.

"After a great deal of bargaining over the silk, we came away without it, but the next day the Chao

Chom sent us back to buy it at the merchant's price. To my surprise, he left five ticals in my hand when I paid him.

"One of the other slave women took it quickly. I said nothing—I had no interest in such profits—and the merchant looked at me keenly. The Chao Chom sent us back to his shop many times, and the merchant invariably left us five ticals, which the other women always took.

"Because I wore a headscarf, he knew I was a Moslem, as he was. He began to watch me closely, though always with respect, and I could not help but notice that his face was kind. One day after we made a purchase he left twenty ticals on the floor beside me. My companions pointed to the money, but I would not take it. When the merchant saw my unwillingness, he picked up fifteen ticals and left five.

"We returned by the river as was our custom. Every moment of freedom was sweet to us and we paddled our canoe very slowly. I hated to go back to the Palace. I was even tempted to plunge into the water and escape, but the responsibility of the money made me hesitate. Still almost unconsciously I had begun to indulge the hope of obtaining my freedom. I didn't know how or when."

She paused, resuming her tale with a kind of wistful sadness.

"Gracious lady, we all love Allah and we are loved of him. And yet he has made some masters and some slaves. Strange as it may seem to you, the more impossible my hope of freedom became, the more I longed for it. Then one day a slave woman came to my mistress with some new goods. When she saw me she asked for a drink of water. As I handed it to her, she whispered, 'You are a Moslem. Free yourself from bondage to this unbelieving race! Take the price of your redemption from my master! Come out of the Inner Palace and be restored to the true people of God!'

"I listened in astonishment. She left me suddenly, as if she were afraid of having said too much or of having aroused the suspicions of my mistress. I was in a more disturbed state of mind than I had ever been before. My thoughts flew hither and thither like birds during a storm. I found comfort only in trusting to Allah.

"When I saw the woman a second time I asked her, 'How shall I get my purchase money? Tell me quickly!'

"She answered, 'My master will give you the money, and never repent having freed a Moslem and the daughter of a believer from slavery.' I threw my arms around her, shaking with joy. Taking some money from her scarf, she tied it into mine. Then she left me without another word. I was terrified for fear I would be caught with the money in my possession, so I came here that night and hid it under the pavement on which we are sitting.

"Several weeks later we were sent again to the merchant's shop. I had never been so conscious of the shabbiness of my clothes as I was that day. We made our purchases and paid the money. When I stood up to go, my friend the slave woman, whose name was Damni, beckoned to me. Her master followed us into an inner chamber and said—I remember every word—'L'Ore, you are so guileless and so beautiful! Here is the money you have just paid me, double the price of your freedom. Take it, and forget not your deliverer!'

"'May Allah prosper you!' Damni said in awe. But I could say nothing. All I could do was burst into tears. The merchant smiled as if he understood, and went back into the shop, while Damni found a handkerchief and dried my eyes. From that time on I lived from day to day, waiting and hoping. Physical freedom seemed to be almost within my grasp.

"I bided my time like a mother watching for the return of an only child. I knew that I could not persuade the Chao Chom to grant me my freedom unless she was in the mood for it, since she was proud and haughty and I was useful to her. So I waited long and anxiously, praying to God every day, praying only for freedom.

"One day the Chao Chom was so kind to me that I thought my opportunity had come at last. I threw myself at her feet, and said, 'Gracious lady, be merciful and hear my prayer. Accept the price of my freedom, gracious lady. Be merciful! Set me free!'

"I didn't dare to look at her face, and when she spoke I knew that she was angry. She reviled me for ingratitude. She reviewed all her kindnesses to me, all the care and teaching that had been lavished upon me, and accused me of selfishness. I begged and implored and wept.

"'You were born my slave,' she said coldly, 'and I will not take money for you. You are much more valuable to me than money.'

"I begged harder. I laid the money before her three times, as is the custom, and pleaded with her to accept it. 'Take double, most honored and gracious lady, only let me go!'

"'Never!' she screamed in a terrible voice. 'Be still at once! I'll never set you free!' And then as if she had guessed half of my thought she asked suddenly, 'Do you wish to be married? Is that it? Very well, I'll find you a good husband, and you shall bear me children as your mother did before you. Pick up your money and go, or I'll order you flogged!'

"So it was all in vain. I gathered up my silver and returned to my slave's life, doing my best to appear obedient and cheerful. The Chao Chom gradually took me into her confidence again, although she never let me go out of the Palace, and arranged a marriage for me with Nai Thim, one of her favorite male slaves. I didn't object, for I had made up my mind to escape. I even pretended that I was happy at the prospect of being free to spend six months of every year with my husband.

"The day before my marriage I was sent to see Nai Thim's mother with a small gift from my mistress. Two strong women accompanied me. I had hidden my purchase money in my clothing. As soon as we entered my future mother-in-law's house, I asked permission to speak to her in private. She thought that I had some communication from the Chao Chom and took me to the back of the house, which faced the river. Without giving her time to ask any questions, I told her my whole story. Then I took the money and shoved it into her hands. And before she could refuse it I plunged into the river. I heard one startled scream above me as I disappeared under the water.

"I am a good swimmer, and I swam for my life. The current took me rapidly downstream. I came to the surface from time to time for air, and then dived back under. The old lady's house was far below the

Palace and there were no boats there as there are here in the heart of the city. When I found my strength failing I made for the opposite bank and climbed its steep sides. There were no houses about and I was sure that no one had seen me from the moment I sank below the water. The old lady would think that I had drowned myself and the slaves would go back to the Chao Chom with her story. She, too, would count me dead. I had accomplished what had been the beginning and end of all my thoughts for two years. It seemed to me at first that perhaps it was a dream. Then I knew it was not, and my joy was so great that I laughed out loud, and danced, and sang.

"From day to day my soul had been slowly withering away. Now it blossomed forth afresh and I could do nothing but rejoice. I do not know how many hours I sat there, but they were as minutes. Suddenly the sun set. The night descended. The wind began to blow in fitful gusts. I knew that there were angels who heard the cries of human distress. So I prayed to them to come and hover near me, and as I prayed a deep sleep came upon me."

She paused again, musing. "I had been dazzled with the idea of liberty. But as dawn came I was faced with the question: Where shall I go? Who will employ me? There was no one in all this vast city to whom I could turn but the merchant and his slave woman.

"Damni had told me how to find her, and now I set off along the riverbank. I was hungry and frightened, yet full of resolve. Keeping out of sight, I walked all day. At twilight I stumbled into her hut, footsore and weary. Damni was overjoyed to see me. She fed me, gave me fresh clothing, and provided me with shelter.

"Soon after, the merchant came to visit. He proposed marriage."

L'Ore's voice trembled with emotion. "At first I could not believe that a prosperous merchant would marry an outcast slave like me. But I accepted his proposal, and the next day Damni dressed me in a white sari and accompanied me to the Mullah's house. There the merchant and I were wed.

"During the days that followed I was as one drunk with new wine. I thanked Allah for the sun, for the beautiful summer days, the radiant yellow sky. I thanked him for the freshness of dawn and for the dew of evening. The glory of God shone upon me and filled my soul with intense delight. It blossomed like a garden of flowers in the perfect pattern of happiness.

"One day, about three or four months after my marriage, as I was sitting on the steps of my home, I thought I heard a voice in my ear. I had hardly time to turn when I was seized, gagged, bound hand and foot, and brought here. When I was taken into the presence of my mistress, she ordered me chained to this post. Here I was chained until my time came and my child was born. A month after his birth I was chained here again, and my child was brought to me to nurse. This was done until he could come to me alone. But they are not unkind. When it is very wet the slave woman takes him to sleep under the shelter of her little shed."

L'Ore's voice had become feeble and almost inarticulate. "I could free myself from these chains if I would promise never to quit the Palace. That I will not do." Her head drooped on her breast. Then she fell forward on the stones, her hands clasped, her face buried in the dust. Anna knelt quickly beside her, but it was not a faint. She had fallen into a sort of stupor.

Anna looked at the woman lying on the pavement before her and marveled. The rudeness of her appearance, the sun-parched skin, the unkempt hair! Four years of unremitting cruelty, of exposure to sun and wind and rain, had not dimmed her courage or broken her spirit. Yet how much more could she endure? Anna had the awe-struck feeling that she herself was the answer to L'Ore's impassioned prayers. Else how had she come to the brass door? Perhaps her seemingly aimless wanderings had had direction.

Anna reached down and touched L'Ore softly on the shoulder. The slave asked if she had been dreaming. Her mind seemed to be in a daze. Anna, looking deeply into L'Ore's eyes, gave up any attempt to comfort her with promises. Action alone would help her, and it was impossible to tell what could be done.

She left the slave face down on the burning pavement and passed through the silent door. The long, dark street was empty as before.

After twenty minutes of straying in and out of the harem streets Anna found one that was familiar. When she reached the schoolroom it was twelve o'clock and her pupils were all in their places waiting for her.

FOURTEEN

A SLAVE IS FREED

When school was over that afternoon Anna set out to find the merchant who had been L'Ore's husband. The shops of the Moslem cloth merchants were all in one small section of the city, and she had no trouble finding his. L'Ore had told her that his name was Ibrahim. It was a prosperous shop, full of rich silks, perfumes, altar candles, and scented tapers. The merchant was a tall Indian with kind eyes. Anna asked to speak to him privately and was taken into the

apartment at the back of the shop. When she told him that she had come from his wife and child in the Palace, he was at first overjoyed to know that they were both alive and then moved to tears by their distress.

That night a group of Moslems called on Anna. Together they drew up a petition addressed to the King, which Anna agreed to deliver the next morning. The same invisible power that had drawn her to L'Ore seemed to be working still, for she was summoned early to the King's presence. She carried the petition with her and a gift, a small book entitled *Curiosities of Science*. The King was very much pleased with the book and very gracious as she handed him the petition. He read it carefully, and then gave it back to her saying, "Inquiry shall be made by me into this case." The next day she received a note from him:

> *Lady Leonowens:—I have liberty to do an inquiry for the matter complained, to hear from the Princess Phra Ong Butri, the daughter of the Chao Chom Manda Ung, who is now absent from hence. The princess said that she knows nothing about the wife of Naikodah, but that certain children were sent her from her grandfather maternal, that they are offspring of his maid-servant, and that these*

children shall be in her employment. So I ought to
see the Chao Chom Manda Ung, and inquire from
herself.

    S.S.P.P. Maha Mongkut, R.x.

His Majesty was as good as his word. As soon as
the Chao Chom returned, he ordered the chief of the
female judges, Anna's friend Khun Thao Ap, to make
an investigation. This turn of events pleased Anna,
since she knew the judge to be just. By the King's
order Anna carried the petition to the judge. She
found her in an open *sala* that formed one side of the
prison and was her court. As Anna entered, the judge
raised her eyes from the scroll of the law that she had
been studying.

"Ah, it is you, Mem," she said, taking off her spectacles. "I wish to speak to you."

Anna was almost as much in awe of this stern
woman as were the ladies of the harem, but she said
boldly, "And I have something to lay before you also."

"Yes, I know. You have a communication to make
to me that has already been presented to His Majesty.
Well, your request is granted."

"Granted! How?" Anna asked in astonishment. "Is
L'Ore already free to leave the Palace?"

"Oh, no! But His Majesty's letter gives us the
authority to proceed against the Chao Chom. These

great ladies will not come in person unless they are summoned by a royal letter like this one," she explained. "They merely send frivolous excuses and stay away."

When she saw that Anna was still puzzled, the judge explained what L'Ore had already tried to explain, that the Chao Chom was not only a consort of the late King, but the daughter of one of the great families of Bangkok. Her position as a dowager queen and her family's influence at court were such that she was immune to any but the King's specific orders, which of course were law for everyone. Her only daughter, Princess Butri, had been the teacher of the late queen, and was thus a privileged person. In addition, she was much admired as an authority on Palace etiquette and as a fine poet.

Anna smiled at the last words. She had been right, then, in her guess that L'Ore's manner of speech was not an accident, but the result of her education. The judge sent a sheriff to summon the Chao Chom, the princess, and the slave woman. Two hours later the dowager consort and the princess appeared, accompanied by an immense group of female slaves.

The great ladies, who were both small and fine-boned, took their places on embroidered velvet cushions. There was an air of authority about them, and a subdued insolence in their manner toward the judge.

But the judge was unimpressed. The soft eyes in her heavy face were aloof. Only her graceful hands adjusted her spectacles as if better to see the women before her. She looked at the great ladies for a moment and asked, "Where is the slave woman, L'Ore?" The dowager cast a malicious glance at the judge, but did not answer. In the silence of the court her unspoken defiance echoed more loudly than words.

Around the open *sala* a group of slave women and children had collected, crouching on their heels. Anna was deeply moved by the expression on their faces. One of their humble number had challenged the great ladies of the Palace, and they hardly dared to believe that she could succeed in gaining her freedom. They all knew her story.

They saw the contempt on the faces of the queen dowager and her daughter. They looked from them to the severe face of the judge with anxious concentration, trying to fathom her expression. The Chao Chom had openly defied the judge. What would the judge do? Hope burned in unblinking eyes as they watched her, for they knew that the dark stern woman before them was just and fair. She had as much respect for the rights of the humblest as for those of the queen dowager herself.

The judge read aloud, in a clear voice, the letter she had received from the King. When it was finished the dowager and her daughter saluted the letter by prostrating themselves three times before it. Then the judge asked the ladies, "Can you advance any reason why the slave woman L'Ore should not be freed when she has offered to pay the full price of her freedom?"

Every eye in the crouching throng fastened on the face of the queen dowager. She spoke with difficulty, struggling to control the rage that shook her. "The slave L'Ore was born in bondage. We do not choose to free her, since she has been useful to our daughter."

The judge looked sterner, more impassive. She ignored the calculated discourtesy of the other woman and spoke in a slow, measured voice: "It is the law and custom of this country that bond servants have the right to redeem themselves if they wish, and if they have the money with which to do it."

"And what if every slave in my service should bring me the price of her freedom?" cried the Chao Chom.

All eyes turned to the judge; every ear strained to catch her reply. "Then, lady," she said with quick emphasis, "you would be bound to free every one of them. That is the law."

"And serve myself?" screamed the dowager.

The voice of the judge was as cool as a lake. "Even so, my august mistress," she said, bowing low.

A sigh escaped the crowd. The Chao Chom turned very pale and trembled slightly. The judge went on in her measured tones, ignoring both the mounting excitement of the slaves and the blazing anger of the royal ladies. "The bond servant L'Ore desires to be free. It is the wish of the royal governess to redeem her, and His Majesty's pleasure that this shall be done in accordance with the Law of Servitude. I therefore declare and decree that the bond servant L'Ore is no longer the slave of the Chao Chom. I do further decree that the price of her redemption shall be set at forty ticals."

The dowager looked at Anna spitefully. "Let her purchase money be paid now, and she is freed from my service forever."

Anna was distressed. She had not brought that much money with her. But the judge spoke directly to her as if the pettiness of the dowager were a small matter not worth her attention. "You are now the mistress of L'Ore. I will have the *dika* papers made out. Bring the money to me tomorrow and all will be arranged."

"Thank you! Thank you very much." Anna rose from the floor, her knees stiff and shaky. She bowed coldly to the great ladies but they ignored her. This troubled her not at all, for her heart was full, and she returned home radiantly happy.

The next day she presented herself at court again. The judge handed her the *dika* that freed L'Ore and ordered one of the female sheriffs to go with her to see the money paid, and L'Ore liberated.

Once more Anna went through the tortuous alleys that ended at the brass door. Her heart was beating wildly as she pushed it open and stepped within. There was the slave, chained as before. But the piazza of the deserted house was full of people. Anna's heart leaped in triumph. The princess and the Chao Chom sat there, surrounded by their sympathizing women. They pretended to be unaware of Anna's presence, but they had not dared to be absent.

The sheriff was timid and hesitant, so obviously afraid of her official duty, that Anna finally advanced alone. She opened her purse and took out forty pieces of silver money. She had hardly laid them before the dowager when the angry woman dashed them away with her foot contemptuously. Anna ignored this childishness and kept her eyes fixed on the woman's face. Grudgingly the dowager gave the order that L'Ore was to be released and allowed to go.

A female blacksmith, a dark and heavy woman, moved to the side of the slave and removed her chains. L'Ore was free at last! To Anna's amazement she did not move. When her chains fell off she merely sank to the pavement and lay inert with her hands folded before her royal persecutors. Anna stepped forward and spoke to her, but L'Ore made no sound. It was as if the chains had fallen from her leg but not from her mind, leaving her as helpless as before.

The thought had come to Anna when she had first talked to L'Ore that her long ordeal might have affected her mind, so that even physical freedom would not restore her. She could not drag L'Ore away by force, yet to leave her there would be a terrible humiliation as well as a serious defeat of justice, and the death of hope in many hearts.

She whispered, "What is the matter? What has gone wrong?" But the timid sheriff cast down her eyes and did not answer.

Anna was profoundly troubled. She felt, as she often did in the harem, that she was walking on quicksand. The royal women on the piazza were chattering busily. Meanwhile, L'Ore lay like one dead, her brown back burned to ebony by the sun, her matted hair fallen over her outstretched arms. As Anna stood, determined not to be driven away or outwitted, a woman with a child in her arms passed behind her and whispered, "They have taken away her child."

So that was it! She had not foreseen this maneuver. The royal ladies had planned cleverly and maliciously. Free the slave they must, since the King had ordered it. But nothing had been said about the child. The faces in the crowd were marked with sympathy and sadness, as if the miracle of L'Ore's freeing had been too much to hope for after all. Anna caught faint, half whispered sighs. Then the same woman said in her ear, "Go back! Demand to buy the child!"

There was nothing else to do. She went back, alone and sad, more than half afraid that the case was lost. L'Ore would not leave her son, and Anna did not know whether there was any hope for him in the law or not.

The judge was still sitting on her strip of matting in the court when Anna reached it and stated her case. She said nothing, but opened a casket, drew out a scroll and started toward the house of the brass door, where the scene was just as Anna had left it. There sat the royal ladies, holding small jeweled hand mirrors and creaming their lips with a sublime air of indifference. There lay L'Ore, still lying before them, her face hidden on the pavement. As Anna and the judge appeared, the crowd of slave women pressed in, straining to see what the judge would do.

She bowed courteously to the ladies and opened the scroll to read the law: "If any woman have children during her bondage, they shall be slaves also, and she is bound to pay for their freedom as well as for her own. The price of an infant in arms is one tical, and for every year of his life shall be paid one tical."

This declaration produced no effect whatsoever on

the royal ladies, but a strong one on the crowd of slave women. One after another they pressed coins into Anna's hand, until she had the price of the child. She laid the four ticals down in front of the Chao Chom and the princess, who would not acknowledge them—or her. The judge, seeing that they intended to do nothing about restoring the child to his mother, sent one of the sheriffs for the boy.

In half an hour he was in his mother's arms. She did not start with surprise, but turned up to heaven a face that was joy itself. Both mother and child bowed before the great ladies, who pretended not to notice them. Then L'Ore tried to stand up and walk, and failing at first, laughed at her own awkwardness. Eager hands pulled her to her feet and she limped and hobbled away, borne along by the exulting crowd, at whose head marched the judge. Her weakness and difficulty in walking did not lessen her radiance. With her face pressed close to her boy's, she talked to herself and to him: "How happy we shall be! We, too, have a little garden in your father's house. My Thuk will play in the garden. He will chase butterflies in the grass, and I will watch him all day long."

The keepers of the gate handed flowers to the boy as L'Ore and Anna passed through, saying, *"Phutho di chai nak na! Di chai nak na!"* (Merciful Buddha, we are very glad indeed! Very, very glad indeed!)

In some mysterious way the news had spread outside the Palace. Before Anna, L'Ore, and Thuk had more than stepped through the gates on their way to the river they were surrounded by a host of Malays, Indians, Siamese, and Chinese, who had loosened pieces of their clothing and converted them into flags.

So with an army of many-colored banners flying, the men, women, and children running and shouting along the banks of the Chow Phya, L'Ore and her son were put into a boat that took them down the river to their home.

The next day the merchant called on Anna to repay the money she had advanced for his wife and child, and to tell her that his son's name of Thuk, or "Sorrow," had been changed to "Free."

FIFTEEN

THE DEATH
OF THE FA-YING

The effect of L'Ore's almost miraculous return to her husband was far-reaching. Slaves going into the city from the Palace on business told the story to shopkeepers, who passed it on to their customers. Some of the great ladies of the Inside complained bitterly to their families outside. They were frightened by the thought that a slave could demand and get freedom merely because the price of it was available. Their fortunes and their comfort depended

upon the possession of hundreds of slaves. From that time forward Anna had powerful enemies among the nobility who suspected her of revolutionary ideas.

To the common people she became a heroine—the "White Angel." When she entered the temple schoolroom she found on her chair flowers plucked by slaves' hands and woven into garlands. It was as if the humble people of Palace and city had lifted their heads in hope of something better.

A week after L'Ore was freed, the attention of the court swung away to other things. The King and those about him were deeply involved with the cremation of one of the King's sons. The cremation was to be on a grand scale, and school had been dismissed for a week so that the royal children might attend. Anna was glad to have a little time to catch up on her personal correspondence and teach Louis. It so happened, then, that both of them were at home on the afternoon of May 14. Louis called out, "Look, Mama, look!" and pointed up the river toward the Palace. One of the royal barges had shot out into the midst of the river traffic and was coming toward them with tremendous speed. The boats of the market people gave way hurriedly for the barge.

The moment it had come alongside the quay a slave ran to Anna with a letter bearing the King's seal. Anna broke it open and read:

My dear Mam,—

Our well-beloved daughter, your favorite pupil, is attacked with cholera, and has earnest desire to see you, and is heard much to make frequent repetition of your name. I beg that you will favor her wish. I fear her illness is mortal, as there has been three deaths since morning. She is best beloved of my children.

I am your afflicted friend,
S.S.P.P. Maha Mongkut.

And the slave added an entreaty. "My lady," she cried, "three slaves are lying dead in the princess's court. And the Fa-ying was seized this morning. She keeps crying out for you. Please come to her quickly!"

Anna stopped only long enough to tell Louis that he must stay with Beebe, and go nowhere at all, and eat nothing but what Beebe cooked, and then she was in the barge. There was a coldness around her heart and her hands were wet with sweat. The boat seemed to crawl across the river. She learned that the little princess had gone with several other of the royal children to the theatricals and fireworks which were part of the cremation festivities, on the evening before. She had seemed perfectly well. There had been cholera in the city for some weeks past, as there was every year, but no one had thought much about it, since the epidemic was not serious.

"Can't you go a little faster?" Anna urged the rowers, but they were already exerting themselves to the limit of their strength. The current seemed to shove against them, and when Anna reached the heavy gates they opened with incredible slowness. She was breathless when she reached the little princess's room. Dr. Campbell from the British Consulate was the first person she saw. "She is dying," he told her sadly.

The Fa-ying lay on a mattress in the middle of a carpet, under a canopy hung with mosquito netting. Around her bed relatives and slaves were chanting in anxious urgency, "Phra Arahan! Phra Arahan!" the most sacred of the titles of Buddha, which is repeated in the ears of the dying to remind the soul to go to heaven and not to lose its way. Old Princess Lamom, who had raised the child, was kneeling on the floor at her feet, too overcome to do more than whisper the sacred words.

Not this child! Anna's heart protested. Of all the children in the Palace, surely not this one child! The Fa-ying opened her eyes. Recognition stirred. She held out her arms. Anna flew to her, picked her up, and held her tight against her breast. The Fa-ying nestled close to her with a faint sigh, and lay still.

Anna closed her own eyes in a vain effort to press back the tears. When she looked down again, the Fa-ying was dead.

Anna kissed the delicate face, thinking with a sharp spasm of grief that there was no more need for the chant now. This little one would never lose her way again. She laid the tiny body on the mattress and straightened up. The meaning of what she had done reached those in the room. The death chant was succeeded by a sudden burst of wailing. The sound rose through the afternoon air and was caught up by others of the harem who were kneeling on the pavement outside. Anna could hear the shrill lament echo and re-echo faintly through the streets of the Inside as word was passed along.

"Dr. Bradley and I did everything we could," Dr. Campbell said heavily as he leaned down and picked up his bag. "It was already too late when they called us. Her pulse was faint and her skin was cold." He sighed, looked at Anna briefly and went out.

Anna was stunned by the swiftness of the cholera. Only yesterday the Fa-ying had been alive and happy. Just a few short hours ago she had embodied all that was dear to her royal father and many of her teacher's hopes for the future. Now she was gone. One of the women in charge begged Anna to carry the terrible news to the King. None of them dared to tell him that his favorite child was dead. Anna agreed when she saw that the panic of the women was real.

Attendants conducted her to door of his study. He was sitting apart, still dressed in the white garments he had worn to the cremation of his son. He had just returned from lighting the pyre. As Anna entered the room she searched her mind for words with which to break the news to him. She could find none, but she did not need any. He read her face, and covering his own with his hands, wept passionately.

What could she say? There was nothing. She sat helpless and yet unwilling to go, leaving the King alone with his grief. It was late afternoon and the last of the sunlight slanted through the windows. The great clock on the nearby tower tolled six. The King sat with his head sunk in his hands, mourning for his child, murmuring her name as if the Fa-ying were still there on his knee. Tears streamed down Anna's cheeks as she listened. So for an hour they sat almost without speaking. And during that time they were not an English schoolteacher and a haughty Eastern monarch, but a man and a woman weeping together for a beautiful child they had both loved. Then Anna stole quietly away.

It was morning before the King was able to go to the hall where the Fa-ying's body lay, on a white satin cushion fringed with heavy gold. In the quiet room all were weeping. With trembling lips the royal father took the little body in his arms and bathed it in the ceremonial manner by pouring cold water over it.

In this he was followed by other members of the royal family, and by relatives of the princess, and by the ladies-in-waiting. Each advanced in the order of her rank and poured water from a silver bowl over the slender body. Two sisters of the King then shrouded it in a sitting posture, wrapping it tightly in long strips of waxed cloth, overlaid it with perfume, frank-incense, and myrrh, and swaddled it in a fine winding sheet.

When these preparations were complete each person crept to the body and took a formal leave of it by repeating, *"Pai sawan na! Chao-fa-ying cha."* (Go now to heaven, Chao-fa-ying.) After the leave-taking was over, three young girls dressed in white brought two golden urns. The body was gently deposited in the first and this in turn was placed in the second, which was of finer gold and richly adorned with precious stones.

The double urn was placed on a gilt sedan and borne under a royal umbrella to the temple of the Dusit Maha Prasat, where it was mounted on a platform six feet high and surrounded with lighted tapers, tall candles, and fragrant oil lamps which hung from the ceiling. These lights would burn night and day until the cremation.

The King had followed the body of his favorite child from the Palace with anguish in his face. During the ceremony he sat apart, his head buried in his hands. Insignia pertaining to the rank of the little princess were placed below the urn. Then the musicians struck up a lamentation, ending in a solemn dirge. When this had been completed His Majesty and all the princely company retired, leaving the lovely Fa-ying in the peaceful beauty of the Maha Prasat.

A few days later the same royal barge that had come to summon Anna to the deathbed of the Fa-ying, bearing the same female slaves, came again in haste to her house. His Majesty commanded her presence at once.

"Is someone else ill with the cholera?" she asked in alarm. But they would not say.

When she arrived at the school pavilion she found it decorated with flowers. Her chair had been painted red, and around the back and arms and legs fresh flowers had been twined. The books of the Fa-ying were laid out in order on the table in front of Anna's accustomed place. Across them had been placed a sheaf of roses and lilies.

The women of the harem were bustling about. Some of them whispered to her that an extraordinary honor was about to be bestowed on her. Puzzled and apprehensive, she submitted quietly to being enthroned in the gorgeous chair. The paint was hardly dry, and she groaned inwardly at the thought of the damage to her dress.

In a little while a messenger came from the King to ask whether Anna had arrived. As soon as he knew that she was in her place, he descended from his chambers, accompanied by the great ladies of the harem, the dowagers, his sisters, cousins, and aunts, paternal and maternal.

When he had shaken hands with Anna and Louis, he explained the nature of the occasion. He was about to confer on Anna a distinction that had never been given to any foreigner. It was in consideration of her devoted interest in his daughter, and for her "courage and conduct," as he expressed it, at the deathbed of his well-beloved child. Then, bidding Anna remain seated, he carefully took seven threads of unspun cotton and passed them over her head and over the dead child's books and then placed the end of each single strand in the palm of each of the seven of his elder sisters.

This done he solemnly sprinkled Anna with twenty-one drops of water from a jeweled conch shell while chanting in Sanskrit. Then, handing her a small silk bag, he commanded her to rise Chao Khun Kru Yai— Lord Most Excellent Teacher.

Anna was touched and embarrassed by her new honors, and surprised to find that the bag contained a patent of nobility and the title to many roods of land in the far-off district of Lopburi. To reach her new estate, she learned, she would have to make a long journey through dense jungle on the back of an elephant.

Louis, who longed to ride an elephant through the jungle, was disappointed when Anna decided against it. She explained that she wanted the tigers, elephants, rhinoceroses, wild boars, armadillos, and monkeys who inhabited her land to live free and undisturbed.

"I do not think their happiness depends on meeting us," she told Louis. "In fact, I am sure of it, my dear."

SIXTEEN

THE PRINCE
GROWS UP

When Anna had been in the Palace for almost three years, she decided to ask the King for the increase in salary which he promised to give her long ago when her work increased. There was no doubt that her work had doubled and trebled. She was busy with her school all day and was often summoned to translate in the evening. Her royal pupils showed progress and the King often expressed his pleasure with it. The cost of keeping her little daughter Avis at school in England was three hundred dollars a year, and living in Bangkok was not cheap. There were servants to pay, food to buy, Louis and herself to clothe, all on a hundred dollars a month. And there were the claims upon her of the distressed, who came more and more frequently.

But to her astonishment, when she brought the matter of her salary up with the King, confident that he needed only to be reminded, he turned on her angrily. He said that "she had not given satisfaction," and added that she was "difficult and unmanageable, more careful about what was right and what was wrong than for obedience and submission. And as to salary," he continued, "why you should be poor? You come into my presence every day with some petition, some case of hardship or injustice and you demand, 'Your Majesty shall kindly investigate, and cause redress to be made'; and I have granted to you because you are important to me for translation and so forth. And now you declare you must have increase of salary! Must you have everything in the world? Why you do not make them pay you? If I grant you all your petition for the poor, you ought to be rich, or you have no wisdom."

That ended the argument. The King refused to discuss the matter. Anna was almost made speechless, anyway, by the discovery that the King actually thought she would profit from the miserable souls that came to her for help. She turned away, taking little comfort in the thought that her influence had grown to the point where even the women and children of the Inside looked to her for pity. Many of them, seeing that she was not afraid of the King, imagined that she had powers that were more than human. So not only the poor, but the highly placed ladies of the harem came to her secretly with their troubles. Without meaning to, she found herself set up between the oppressor and the oppressed. Though she tried to excuse herself from interfering, the pleas she heard were often so heartrending that she felt compelled to help. Sometimes she sent Louis to the judges with her "clients," sometimes she went herself. Louis had become a great favorite with the King. He had written Avis: "I like the King. He gave me some gold leaf for you which I send you with all my love." Anna had to admit to herself that justice was granted not from a sense of right, but either through fear of her influence with the King or through Louis's known popularity.

Not all her contacts with the women of the harem were of this sort. She saw the mothers of her pupils on many different occasions and was on excellent terms with most of them. There were a select few to whom she was especially close. They all had a practical concern for those around them, and this attracted her very much.

Lady Son Klin gave Anna valuable assistance in her study of the Siamese language. She was always delighted to see Anna in her home, and would produce hot tea and cakes with a rush of pleased attention that was heartwarming after a tiring day in the schoolroom. Her advice was shrewd and cautious. She understood the intricate politics of the harem and steered her friend through them with diplomatic skill. Anna was saved many a blunder by her careful little warnings.

Anna's relationship with Lady Thiang was almost as intimate, but of quite another sort. She had quickly discovered the greatness of this Siamese woman's heart. Life in the harem was endurable for many of the women of the Inside only because the head wife was a person of broad sympathy and discretion. Anna had often carried some story of distress to her and had always been reassured if Lady Thiang said quickly, "Don't worry any more, Mem *cha*, I'll attend to it myself."

The head wife had made up a little court drama of her own in which she cast Anna for the leading part and used her again and again, with marked success. Whenever Lady Thiang thought that the King was dangerously angry and ready to order one of the women of the harem punished, she would send quickly for Anna. It was Anna's role to go immediately to the room in which His Majesty was, book in hand, to consult him about a translation from the Sanskrit or

Siamese. She kept a supply of such questions ready for these occasions. Simple as this trick was, or perhaps just because it was simple, it worked.

The King would see Anna standing hesitantly at the door with her book and would motion her to come in. Then he would turn with comical abruptness from curses and threats to absorbed interest in the question she raised. The scholar would win over the man. Often he would motion the culprit, still kneeling before him, out of the room with an absent-minded wave of his hand, so that he would be free to devote himself to the interesting problem that Anna had brought him. Again and again as she approached his study and heard his voice harsh with anger, she would feel her heart sink and her steps slow down. This time he would guess! But he never did.

Princess Lamom was the third person whom Anna especially liked. The old princess often sought advice about Prince Chulalongkorn and his brothers after she had recovered sufficiently from her grief over the death of the Fa-ying. Without her cooperation it would hardly have been possible to plant the principles of kindness in Chulalongkorn's mind. Anna made it a point to tell the young Prince about her efforts to help this or that unfortunate person. He listened gravely, his eyes alert and interested. She was convinced that she was having an effect when he began to notice the cruelty with which the slaves were treated in the Palace and talk about it with a troubled look. It was a beginning, she felt, to have opened his eyes to this.

She herself, to use the King's phrase, was "a candle flame blowing in the wind." If she could light one lamp that would some day illuminate every corner of the kingdom, her work in Siam would have been more than worthwhile.

The King had refused to increase her salary, but it was some reward for her efforts when she noticed that the young Prince was trying to teach kindness toward the slaves by his own example. He had his slaves carefully dressed and well fed, and he treated them with consideration. He insisted that his younger brothers and attendants do the same. One day he startled Anna by saying thoughtfully, "I don't think they ought to be called slaves. They have more right to be called noble than we have, because they have learned how to endure. We princes are the ones who haven't learned that there is nothing noble in oppressing our fellow men."

Anna was very conscious during the last months of 1865 that Prince Chulalongkorn was growing up. His wrists hung out of his jacket. The roundness of his face had disappeared and the childish droop of his mouth was gone. He was much taller than he had been and more slender. The little boy she had begun to teach three years earlier was turning into a man.

The whole Palace was busy with preparations for his coming tonsure—a ceremony in which the Prince's hair would be shaved. The Prince was now thirteen and would soon become a novice to the priesthood, since this event must take place before a boy was fourteen. At that time his hair and eyebrows would be shaved in accordance with Buddhist custom. It was therefore important that the long lock of hair which had been kept uncut on top of his head since babyhood should be removed according to the Brahman rite of *Sokan* before it was shaved.

From the day the Prince was born, King Mongkut had been eager to settle the crown on him. According to the laws of the country there was no way that this could be done: the final choice of each new king rested with the council of nobles. King Mongkut was afraid that the council might choose his younger brother, the Second King, and not his son, since there was a strong prejudice against a boy king. The most the King could do was let his wish become known, and in the meantime do what he could to elevate his son in the estimation of the nobility and the people. Now he planned the most elaborate tonsure that he could devise, knowing that ceremonies like this enhanced the importance of his son in the eyes of the people.

The whole royal establishment was set in motion. About nine thousand young women were cast for parts in a mammoth pageant, borrowed partly from the old Indian classic, the *Ramayana*, and partly from the ritual of the kings of Cambodia. The King had had the ancient narrative poem *Kailasa* adapted for the occasion. Boys and girls of good family were brought from all quarters of the kingdom to assist. So vast were the preparations that school suffered. Regular studies had to be abandoned, and in their place were rehearsals of singing, dancing, recitation, and pantomime.

An artificial hill called Mount Kailasa was erected in the center of the Palace gardens. It was fifty feet high and at least three hundred feet around. The wooden framework was shaped to make peaks, valleys, and caves, and covered with bamboo. Over this was laid metallic paper so that parts of the mountain seemed to be made of iron, other parts of copper, brass, tin, silver, or gold. On the summit was a golden temple.

On New Year's Eve—December 31, 1865—monks assembled in the Dusit Maha Prasat to chant while the Brahmans performed their own rites in a specially erected chapel. On each of the three preliminary days the procedure was the same. The mornings were devoted to religious services by the two sets of priests.

In the afternoon the Prince was carried on a platform by a long and roundabout way through the Palace grounds to the Dusit Maha Prasat. Here the King awaited him and together they made offerings of candles and incense before the images. Then in the same platform both King and Prince returned over the same route.

On the fourth of January excitement reached fever pitch, for this was the great day of the actual tonsure. The route to the Maha Prasat was somewhat shortened and the long procession of thousands of people started earlier. Near the temple the Prince was met by a group of girls who held before him tufts of palm and branches of gold and silver. They escorted him to the inner chamber of the temple, where he was seated on a carpet heavily fringed with gold, placed before an altar on which were lighted candles and offerings of many kinds.

All the princes, nobles, and high officers of government, with the Brahman priests who were to oversee the ceremony, and a company of Buddhist priests, musicians, trumpeters, and conch-blowers were assembled. As the priests took up their chant, a Brahman placed a ball of unspun thread in the hands of the Prince. The ends of it were carried around the sacred mountain and then around the temple itself and finally into the inner chamber, where it was bound around the head of the young Prince. From there, nine strands were passed around the altar and into the hands of the head priest. These latter threads, forming circles within circles, were symbols of the mystic word *OM*.

The King poured a few drops of water from a conch shell on the Prince's head, the favorable moment was proclaimed by trumpeters, conch-blowers, and other musicians, and the supreme climax of the ceremony arrived. The royal sire handed to the Brahman priests first the golden shears and then a gilded razor. The long lock of hair that had been growing on the Prince's head since he was a baby was clipped and then his head was shaved.

Anna feared the effect this would all have on the Prince. After all, the tonsure ceremony had employed the energies of people from all over the kingdom as well as the entire personnel of the Palace for months. It had consumed hundreds of thousands of ticals from the royal treasury. The Prince had been the central figure in a court drama that would hardly be equaled in his lifetime. Even if he became king, his coronation would not be as elaborate as his tonsure had been. It would not be surprising if these events were to inflate his ego.

Apparently this was not the case. He was dreamy-eyed and thoughtful during this period, but as quiet and unassuming as he had been before. He was to enter the priesthood in July for three months. Anna's influence over him would end at that time (temporarily at least, and perhaps permanently) and she spent as much time with him as she could during the interval.

From his studies in both English and Sanskrit he had an exalted ideal standard of life. Anna wished that she could spare him the shock of his first contacts with the world outside the Palace, but that was impossible. He had been so sheltered by his father and his aunt that in many ways he was like a small child. Where an English boy of thirteen would have learned the rough and tumble of life in school, he had known only the world of the Palace. And the Palace was a cage, a gold and silken cage, but still a cage.

The Prince seemed to feel vaguely that he had missed something, for he had said recently to Anna that he would rather be poor and earn his living than be king. "It's true," he said thoughtfully, "that a poor man has to work hard to earn his daily bread, but then he is free. And his food is all he has to win or lose. If I could only be a poor boy, I could be perfectly happy, I think."

Anna thought how little the child knew of poverty and its problems. She respected his sincerity and intelligence too much, however, to point out what his own powers of observation would show him later—that the lot of a poor boy in Siam was far from wonderful. The poor boy of whom the Prince was dreaming would be at the beck and call of some great noble all his life. He would be subject to at least three months' service every year, and if he made the mistake of showing great ability, his term of service would be longer. If it became known that he or she had more than ordinary gifts, any talented person could be forced into royal service.

But if the young Prince dreamed of a life of privacy, his father was more than ever determined to pass on the crown to him. The Second King had died on the day following the Prince's tonsure ceremonies. The King no longer had to fear that his brother would take the throne. Almost instantly he changed his plans. He ordered the construction of a palace east of the Royal Palace to which he would retire as soon as Prince Chulalongkorn was old enough to become king, and from which he would direct his son in the role of monarch. In this unusual way he thought he could assure the throne to his son.

Prince Chulalongkorn's entrance as novice to the priesthood was set for July 19. When he emerged at the end of October he would be considered too old to live within the confines of the Inside. Preparations were under way to alter a building close to his father's palace, within the outer but not the inner wall, for his new residence. Princess Lamom was busy getting ready to move and take over its management. There were even rumors that the King had selected his son's first wife, who would be installed in the new residence. It was whispered that the girl chosen was a granddaughter of the Kralahome.

The rite of entering into the priesthood was simple but solemn. On the first day there was a performance of the *Wien-thien*—"the revolving of the candles in blessing." Selected nobles and princes moved around the Prince, keeping their right shoulders always toward him, and as they moved they passed seven golden candlesticks from one to the other. Nine times they moved solemnly around the young Prince, revolving the candles. This ceremony was performed in the Audience Hall before a small company of guests, who later shared a feast.

On the second day the Prince was dressed in costly white robes and ornaments. Earlier that morning his eyebrows and his hair, which had begun to grow in a short brush all over his head, had been shaved. He was taken from his father's palace by a body of priests and brought to the Temple of the Emerald Buddha. On the way his barefoot escort chanted Buddhist hymns. At the entrance to the temple, while the chanting continued, another band of priests took from him his fine robes and dressed him in simple white. Within, the monks were arranged in a double semicircle, each with a lighted candle in his folded palms. The Prince advanced humbly toward the high priest in the center of the semicircle with his back to the altar, and bowed three times asking to be admitted to the Order. The high priest received him and with their hands interfolded, one upon the other, the Prince vowed to renounce the world with all its cares and temptations, and to observe with obedience the rules of the priesthood. This done, he was dressed in the yellow robes of the Order, instructed briefly in his duties, and the ceremony was complete.

After breakfast had been served, gifts were presented to the Prince. His father was the first to make a gift, then his brothers, uncles, aunts, and cousins; then the Prime Minister and other high officials; and finally the Chinese and Indian merchants. Most of these gifts were to be turned over by the Prince to the other priests. After the presentation, the Prince's brothers entertained the assembly on a little stage. Dressed in full state costume, loaded with gold and precious stones, they put on a performance of Siamese fencing. A Chinese nobleman took this opportunity to give each of them a gold watch, much to the delight of the children and His Majesty. When it was all over, Prince Chulalongkorn was led from the Palace, which had been his home for almost fourteen years, to the simplicity and severity of monastic life.

SEVENTEEN

A QUARREL
WITH THE KING

August 10, 1866, was another day Anna would
never forget. It began pleasantly enough. Beebe
had found some delicious custard apples in the market,
and Anna and Louis had them for breakfast. The
morning was clear and sweet. There was nothing in
the weather to warn of an approaching storm, nor did

Anna have any idea that the end of her drama with the King was close at hand.

His Majesty sent for her early. "Mem," he said, as she entered, "write a letter at once to tell Sir John Bowring I have changed my mind. I do not want him for ambassador to France. I have decided to send a Siamese ambassador instead."

The King's indecision was too common to arouse Anna's indignation any longer, although she did feel that Sir John was being treated rather shabbily. Some months before, the King had written to him requesting his services as ambassador to the Court of France. This letter had hardly had time to reach England where Sir John was living, and already the King had changed his mind.

Before she had written anything, the King added a further command. She was to explain the change in such a way that the blame for it would fall on the British Consul in Bangkok, Mr. Thomas George Knox, whom the King did not like. Or, if she did not want to do this, explain it in some other way, any way she liked so long as she justified the King's course without insulting Sir John. Why not say that the advice was her own?

Anna jumped up from her chair. "Your Majesty," she exclaimed, "I'll do nothing of the sort!" She had expected him to be angry, for he did not like to be crossed, but she had not expected that his anger would be so intense. He tried to beat down her resistance by shouting at her, and when this failed, by threatening her with punishment. She stood up, then, and without replying, walked out of the Palace, across the commons, and into her home.

The pleasant coolness of the morning had been replaced by gathering heat. The air had become damp, and every now and then a rumble of distant thunder reached Anna's ears. No breeze stirred the heavy air. The parched trees and leaves drooped. Nervous and upset by her quarrel with the King, she began to wish more and more that she had left Siam as her friends had been urging her to do. If she had not been so deeply absorbed in her work, particularly in the education of young Prince Chulalongkorn, she would have gone long ago. She had been held by the knowledge of her influence over him. Now that he had entered the priesthood (although for only a brief time), there was no certainty that she would be permitted to continue teaching him after the three months had passed. Perhaps it would be better to go to England with Louis as soon as it could be arranged, and give up the unequal battle with the King.

In the late afternoon the King's private secretary appeared with a paper. He was accompanied by a group of slaves from the Palace. On the paper were a number of accusations that she was to read, acknowledge, and sign, for him to take back to the King. She was also to admit that she was guilty of ingratitude, and atone to the King by following his wishes in the matter of the letter to Sir John Bowring. The accusations were many:

1. She had stolen a valuable Sanskrit book from his library.

2. She had often disobeyed the King's commands.

3. She had thwarted his wishes.

4. She had scolded His Majesty for certain matters of conduct, which were not her concern.

5. She had shown him disrespect by standing while he was seated, thinking evil of him, slandering him, and calling him wicked.

6. She had walked over the head of His Majesty.

7. She had favored the British Consul, Mr. Thomas George Knox, at the expense of the American Consul, Mr. James Madison Hood. In support of this last charge—she had written the American Consul's name at the bottom of a royal notice, after carefully displaying her own and the British Consul's at the top of it.

Anna read the ridiculous accusations, her anger swelling. How the King could hold a grudge! How easily he forgot faithful service! Once, long ago, before she understood Palace etiquette, the King had expressed a desire for a certain book. She had remembered that it was in the room above where His Majesty had been working earlier in the day, and, supposing that she was obeying his wish, she had hurried upstairs after it. Without thinking about it, she had entered a room directly over the one in which the King was sitting, found the book and brought it downstairs. She had expected him to be pleased, but she had "walked over his head." To her surprise the attending women were shaking in terror. With trembling lips they had assured her that if she ever committed such a breach of royal etiquette again she would be cast into a dungeon.

The other charges were equally ridiculous. She handed the strange document back to Phra Alak without a word.

"But you haven't signed it," he noted.

"No, and I never will," she replied curtly. "You can tell the King so."

The slaves all dropped on their knees and begged her, in the names of their various mistresses, to yield to the King's demand and do what he required. She realized that they acted out of love for her, but she would not agree to do what she could not. Phra Alak, who was a man of resources, offered Anna a substantial bribe. No doubt the money had been collected by the women of the Palace for just this possibility, since he could hardly have had so large a sum himself.

"Phra Alak," Anna said reproachfully, "you know perfectly well that I can't be bribed. If what the King asked me to do were right, I'd do it without money. But it's wrong, and I won't do it, and certainly not for money."

After Phra Alak and the other slaves had gone, Anna was so exhausted that she could hardly eat her dinner. The rain had not come and the atmosphere was still oppressive. Little puffs of breeze and occasional thunder held a promise of relief but no drops fell. After dinner she sat alone in her downstairs living room, unable to stop thinking about the events of the day. Her fears were increased by an anonymous note from the Palace telling her that the King's anger had been flamed by her refusal to sign the paper he had sent. He had shouted to the assembled courtiers, "Will no one rid me of this woman?" Anna called her servants and had the doors locked and barred. She told them they were to admit no one, not even from the Palace, unless she ordered them to do so. Anna knew that some of the courtiers were jealous of her, and that the privileged class of nobles hated her for helping slaves. If the King had actually suggested that he would be glad to be rid of her, was she foolish to be afraid? Wasn't it possible that there was at least one of them who would hire an assassin to carry out the King's will?

The storm which had been gathering all day now burst in fury. For three hours, thunder, lightning, and rain were all that could be seen or heard. When the storm ended at last, well after midnight, Anna went up to her room. Should she go to school the next day? She was too tired to decide even that simple question, and went to bed.

She awoke the next morning unrefreshed. After careful thought she decided that it would be better to continue with her normal routine as if nothing had happened. Whenever she was absent her star pupil, Prang, carried on very well. But if she did not go to school, her failure to appear would be reported to the King and might lead him to believe that he had succeeded in frightening her. Anna had schooled herself to resist the appearance of weakness on the ground that her position and even her safety depended upon her ability to always show a cool and confident front.

She started out with Louis at the regular time and passed quickly within the wall of the Palace. A crowd of poor slaves, who lived outside the royal confines, were squatting near the inner gate waiting for it to open. They knew her well and greeted her with profound salaams. Lounging about the gate was a group of soldiers and rough-looking men whom Anna had never seen there before. It was broad daylight. Nervous as she was, there was nothing about them to frighten her except their uncivil appearance. She walked toward them confidently, never doubting that they would give way before her. Instead, the whole group rushed at her, shouting threats and thrusting her back violently. Many of them threatened to throw stones. Anna was too taken by surprise to feel anything. She saw the jagged pieces of rock, the upraised arms, and knew she would experience their impact against her face and body almost immediately.

Then suddenly she was surrounded by a warm rush of humanity. The crowd of slaves had leaped to her defense. They pressed close to her and Louis on all sides, putting their own bodies between them and their attackers. They began to edge her away from the gate. Still close around her and Louis, they accompanied them out of the Palace and to their home, where they pushed them through the door, and shouted to the servants to come quickly. A few minutes more and all the doors and windows were locked and barred.

As the shock wore off, Anna found herself very much shaken. Beebe hovered around her, never leaving her alone in a room. At lunch she tried to eat in order to reassure Louis, who was still frightened, but she found it hard to keep from dropping her knife and fork. The water glass trembled in her fingers. Whenever Anna looked through the slats of the shutters she could see people idling near the house. Several men squatted for more than an hour at the edge of the road not far from her front door. She thought she saw someone hiding in the bushes near the window. A few people came boldly to the door and knocked, but she had forbidden her servants to let anyone in.

Her first impulse was to write to the British Consul and tell him what had happened. She hesitated for several reasons. She had never yielded to the temptation to depend on the Consul's protection in her dealings with the Siamese. It would look cowardly to do so now. She did sit down at her desk and prepare a letter, in which she explained all that had happened—her quarrel with the King; his rage at her behavior; the assault of the men at the gate; and the fact that strange people were lurking near her house. She sealed and addressed the letter, ready to send it if an attack were made on her or the house. Then she had one of her servants go for a carpenter to install iron bars at all the windows, so that the house could resist entry long enough to send for help.

After that she wrote to Captain John Bush, the harbor master, who had befriended her on her first night in Siam so long ago, and who was still her friend. The royal notice referred to in the King's list of accusations had been in Captain Bush's hands. It had, as the King said, annoyed the American Consul very much. Mr. James Madison Hood had come to Bangkok only the fall before, and he was extremely careful to maintain the dignity of his position. He had been insulted to have his name written at the bottom of the circular while the British Consul's and Mrs. Leonowens's names appeared at the top, and he had said so. Anna recalled the incident because she had understood his resentment. Her own name should not have appeared above his. She knew that she had not been responsible for putting it there, and that her handwriting appeared nowhere on the notice. She thought she had a clear memory of whose handwriting did. In her note she asked Captain Bush merely to try to find the notice, if it was still in his possession, since some trouble concerning it had come up between herself and the King.

He arrived that evening, still the cheerful, red-faced friend of her early days in Bangkok. "Here it is, Mem," he said, holding it out to her. Ah, good! She had been right, she saw. "But what do you want it for?" he asked.

"All I want you to do is to take it and give it to the King. Don't ask me why because I'm not going to tell you. Just hand it to him."

Mystified and somewhat amused, he agreed. With difficulty she persuaded the King's secretary, who lived near by, to arrange an immediate audience for Captain Bush.

When Captain Bush was admitted to the King's presence, he handed him the notice, saying simply, "Mem Leonowens tells me that you want to see this."

The King looked at him questioningly, but the smiling Englishman had no explanation, since Anna had given him none. His Majesty took the notice and examined it carefully. His face went blank, then bewildered, then a disgruntled expression appeared. He put his hand to his brow. The handwriting was his own!

"I have forgotten," he said, bewildered.

Captain Bush was back at Anna's house in a short while, chuckling at the King's discomfort. "Now tell me what it was all about," he demanded. And Anna did.

"And was there something about a book that had been lost?" he asked when she had finished.

"Yes," she said, "the King accused me of stealing a book from his library."

"That makes it perfect!" And Captain Bush threw back his head in laughter. "While I was there a little maid came crawling into the room with a book in her hand, and said something about finding it in one of the sleeping apartments. His Majesty looked more upset than ever and made some remark about thinking that you had it. I didn't get the connection."

The Captain had brought assurance from the King that she was forgiven and might come back to work. But Anna hesitated. Surely it would take a little longer for such rage to wear off. She reopened her doors and windows cautiously but she did not enter the Palace for several weeks.

When the *Chow Phya* arrived with foreign mail, the King summoned her. She went quietly, saying nothing. She sat down at her familiar table and began copying the pile of letters that the King had written. After a little while he came into the room and stood at her elbow. She did not look up.

"Mem, you are one great difficulty!" he said in a reproachful tone. "I have much pleasure and favor on you, but you are too obstinate. You are not wise. Wherefore are you so difficult? You are only a woman. It is very bad you can be so strongheaded. Will you now have any objection to write to Sir John and tell him I am his very good friend?"

Anna could not help but smile. "None whatever, Your Majesty," she answered, "if all you want is a letter of good wishes."

She wrote the letter and handed it to him for his signature.

The reconciliation was complete.

EIGHTEEN

"A GOOD AND
TRUE LADY"

Six months later Anna had decided to accompany Louis to England. It had been hard to make the decision, but when it was made she felt relieved. She asked the King for a year's furlough, but the King refused to discuss even the possibility of her leaving Bangkok.

"Mem, you are lazy! You are ungrateful!" he reproached her every time she brought up the matter. Why he should consider her ungrateful, since he had never fulfilled his early promise to raise her salary, it was hard to say. "I have need of you," he argued, and to him that was enough. It took her six months more to win his grudging consent, and even then he would not permit her to go unless she promised faithfully to return quickly. This she could do only conditionally, for she was in poor health. She did not know how long it would take her to recover.

Five years had passed since she had seen her daughter Avis, who was now twelve. Louis, who was only a year younger, needed to be placed in a boarding school with a regular routine. She and Louis had been in the tropics ten hard years and they both needed the colder air of a temperate climate.

However, there were many reasons for Anna to stay. Her influence with the King was greater than it had ever been. Her quarrels with him seemed to have enhanced her position rather than diminished it. And then there were the three hours she had been permitted to spend with Prince Chulalongkorn every evening in his new library. He was not the impressionable child he had been a few months before, but he still responded to her teaching.

There was one occasion during the following

months that Anna was to remember long after. The Prince and she had been talking about the life of Abraham Lincoln. The story of the great President was familiar to the Prince from the constant references she had made to it through the years. On this evening Anna and the Prince were talking about his tragic death. It had made a deep mark on the young Prince's thinking. He leaned across the table, his eyes shining with a determination she would not forget.

"Mem *cha*," he said, "if I live to reign over Siam I shall reign over a free and not an enslaved nation."

Anna looked at the eager face of the boy in front of her and hoped that he would live to accomplish his dream. He was steady and quiet. Unlike his father, who was half of the old world and half of the new, Chulalongkorn was all of the new. He was facing squarely into the future. This was partly Anna's doing and she was glad. Perhaps in this prince, Siam had found an emancipator. Whenever she looked at him and at her other pupils, the new generation, she felt a great hope for the future.

In her final year in Siam, an event occurred which meant more to Anna than any other. On the third of January Lady Son Klin invited Anna to dinner. The invitation itself was not unusual, but the importance Lady Son Klin attached to it was. She kept sending messengers all day reminding Anna of the appointment, and telling her to be sure to come, until Anna was certain she must be planning some very grand entertainment.

After school Anna dressed herself and Louis in their finest. When they arrived, Lady Son Klin had her head and shoulders out the window, looking down the street for them. As they appeared, she rushed to greet them.

Dinner was served in the "study." Fish, rice, jelly, and a variety of sweetmeats came first; then different kinds of vegetables; after them a course of meat, venison, and fowl of all kinds. The meal ended with sweet drinks, preserves, and fruits.

After this truly sumptuous feast the entertainment followed. It was a program of music provided not only by trained slaves but also by Lady Son Klin and her sisters. The air of suppressed excitement that had pervaded the dinner continued. Anna gathered that even the music was only leading up to something else. As it ended, Lady Son Klin rose and led Anna out to her garden.

There in rows knelt all her slaves, one hundred and thirty-two men, women, and children. Each of them was dressed in entirely new garments and seemed to share the same secret excitement that made Lady Son Klin's hand tremble on Anna's arm. Lady Son Klin stood looking down on them from her veranda, smiling at them as they knelt below her, the women in flowered chintz panungs, the men in colors just as bright but without the flowers, the children in the gayest outfits the local markets could provide.

With a shining look at Anna Lady Son Klin began to speak. "I am wishful," she said in her sweet voice, "to be good person. I want never to buy humans again, but only to let go free once and for all. So from this moment I have no more slaves, but hired servants. I give freedom to all of you who have served me, to go or to stay with me as you wish. If you go to your home I am glad. See, here are the papers, which I shall give to each of you. You are free! If you stay with me, I am still more glad. And I will give you each four ticals every month after this day and your food and clothes."

Anna stood silent. There was a lump in her throat. She had been taken completely by surprise. If she had done nothing more than teach this one woman, she knew now that her five hard years had been amply repaid by what she had seen this night.

Anna had put off telling the women and children that she was going until the time was near. The day she made her announcement, she hardly had the courage to face them. For some time they refused to believe she was really leaving. When they could no longer doubt it, they gave her such a demonstration of their love and devotion that she was overcome. Gifts of every sort poured in from all over. Many sent small sums of money to help Anna on the journey. The poorest and humblest slaves brought rice cakes, dried beans, sugar. In vain Anna tried to tell them as gently as possible that she could not take all these things with her. Still the gifts came until she thought she would have enough to provide for the whole ship.

The King himself had been silent and sullen until the morning of her departure. At the end he relented. He embraced Louis and gave him a silver buckle, and a bag containing a hundred dollars to buy sweetmeats on the way. Then turning to Anna, he said: "Mem! you much beloved by our common people, and all inhabitants of Palace and royal children. Everyone is in affliction of your departure. And even that inefficient secretary, Phra Alak, is very low down in his heart because you *will* go. It shall be because you must be a good and true lady. I am often angry on you, and lose my temper, though I have large respect for you. But nevertheless you ought to know you are difficult woman, and more difficult than generality. But you will forget, and come back to my service, for I have more confidence on you every day. Good-bye."

Anna could not reply. Her eyes were full of tears.

She realized that something extraordinary had taken place. She and the King were more than employer and employee, King and governess—they were friends.

He accompanied her to the temple to say farewell to the women and children. They knelt before her, filling the great room, weeping. This was hard enough, but when the King withdrew they were up and around her, embracing her, pressing little notes and last-minute gifts into her hands, reproaching her with tears for leaving them. Anna could stand it no longer. She rushed out and through the gate where they could not follow. But their voices floated after her, the women calling, "Come back! Come back!" and the children, "Mem *cha*, don't go! Don't go away and leave us!"

She hurried to Prince Chulalongkorn for her final and most difficult leave-taking. The prince had written her a little note in his most careful English only a few days before:

Bangkok
July 1st, 1867.

My dear Mrs. Leonowens

I herewith send you a photograph of myself which I trust will meet with your approbation, and which I hope you will keep in remembrance of your pupil, whom you have had the honour of instructing for such a length of time.

Enclosed is a small present of $30 (dollars) for your kind acceptance; and in conclusion I can only wish you a pleasant and quick voyage to Europe, and that you may meet with every enjoyment on your arrival.

I beg to remain
Your faithful friend
Chowfa Chulalongkorn

His regret seemed too deep for words and he managed only a few. Taking both her hands in his own and laying his brow upon them, he said, after a long interval of silence, "Mem *cha*, please come back!"

"Keep a brave and true heart, my prince!" was all that she could say.

Anna and Louis left Bangkok in the steamer *Chow Phya*. Uncertain of the future, she had sold her household goods at auction. All her European friends accompanied her down the river to the Gulf. Then they were alone, she and Louis, on the same ship that had brought them five years before, watching the shore line fade to a thin gray shadow.

NINETEEN

FULFILLMENT

Anna's joy at seeing Avis again was tempered by her doctor's grave diagnosis of her health. The years in the tropics had taken their toll, and he urged her to spend several months in a healthful, temperate climate.

Once Louis had gone off to boarding school in Ireland, Anna moved to the Catskill Mountains in the United States. It was there that a letter came to her

from Siam, with the sad news that King Mongkut had died suddenly on October 1, 1868, after a brief illness.

The King had remembered Anna and Louis generously in his will, but neither of them ever received the inheritance. Nor did Anna return to Siam. The death of the King placed actual power in the hands of the Kralahome, who became regent. The night the King died the Senabodi, or council of ministers, elected Prince Chulalongkorn to succeed his father. The Prince, now fifteen, was crowned on November 11. Everyone who saw him was impressed with his dignity, his quiet assurance, and his lack of arrogance.

He had almost no power and would have none for five years until he had come of age. Nevertheless he was permitted by the Senabodi to proclaim a pardon of all political prisoners. He began at once, quietly and with determination, to set forth his views on the future of the kingdom. His second proclamation established religious freedom. In it he declared:

> *In regard to the concern of seeking and holding a religion that will be a refuge to you in this life: it is a good and noble concern, and it is exceedingly appropriate and suitable that you, as a nation, and each man individually, should investigate for himself, and according to his own wisdom, which is the*

right and which is the wrong; and if you see any
religion whatever, or any body of men professing
any religion whatsoever who seem likely to be an
advantage to you,—a true religion in accordance
with your own wisdom,—hold to that religion with
all your heart. . . .

The question of slavery was more difficult. The
great nobles of the country whose fortunes were based
on the thousands of serfs and slaves at their disposal
feared any attempt to disrupt a system so profitable
to themselves. According to the letters that reached
Anna, young King Chulalongkorn undertook the matter courageously but discreetly. She heard that he had
said to the San Luang, "I see no hope for our country
until it is freed from the dark blot of slavery."

The nobility were impressed by the King's determination, but not persuaded. The Kralahome replied:
"It is impossible to free a nation of slaves without
incurring much risk and danger to the state and to the
slaveholders. Under the existing laws, Siam could not
abolish her system of slavery without undermining at
the same time her whole constitution."

"Well," the King answered, "let it be so for the
time being then. But my slaves, my soldiers, and my
debtors are my own, and I will free them at least,

whatever my ministers may see fit to do. For my part, no human being shall ever again be branded in my name and with my mark!"

After much further discussion the regent and the Senabodi agreed to a gradual end to slavery. The first public pronouncement was made by the King. Standing on the lowest step of his glittering throne before the chief rulers, governors, and judges of the people, he read his declaration:

> *Let this our royal message to our people be proclaimed, and not as if we were doing a great and lordly thing, but our simple duty to our fellowmen and subjects, that from the first day of January, 1872, slavery shall cease to be an institution in our country, and every man, woman and child shall hold themselves free-born citizens; and further let it be made known, that a tax, according to circumstances of each and every man, shall be levied on the nation to remunerate the slaveholders for the loss of their slaves.*

It was to be 1905 before the final proclamation was issued, absolutely and finally ending serfdom and slavery in Siam. The length of time this took was necessary in transforming the country from feudalism to freedom. In the end, however, the King had kept the solemn promise he had made long ago to Anna—"If I live to reign over Siam I shall reign over a free and not an enslaved nation."

Thirty years after she left Siam, Anna Leonowens saw her most distinguished pupil again. She was on her way to Leipzig with the older of Avis's children when King Chulalongkorn arrived in London. She had an interview with him there on August 19, 1897. It was another memorable day in her life.

The King had reigned for twenty-nine years, a grave, quiet, determined man who had accomplished much against great odds. The nobles whose privileges he had restricted had secretly opposed him, but the work of reform had gone on. Schools had been established all over the kingdom. Missionaries had been encouraged in their efforts to start hospitals and schools. Transportation facilities were improved. The law courts had been reorganized. Gradually, educated officials were taking the places of the old feudal administrators. The whole system of government had been reorganized. The military forces were being modernized. Young men were being sent abroad for study, and teachers from Europe and America were being imported. Already in his lifetime the Siamese were beginning to say that Chulalongkorn was their greatest king. When he moved about Bangkok in formal procession, they scattered rice mixed with flowers in his path—their highest tribute.

It was thus with a feeling of deep gratitude and humility that Anna heard him say it was through the principles laid down in her teaching that he had formed the plans by which he had transformed his kingdom. He had kept his determination to recreate a free Siam. It had not been easy. There was much still to do. But in Siam the current of change was running deep and strong and true, full of promise for the future, because it was a change based on the idea of the worth of a human being as Anna had helped instill it into the monarch—a change based on democratic principles.

Anna looked into the future of the country where she had spent the most difficult years of her life and was content.

GLOSSARY

ALLAH In the Islam religion, the name for the one supreme being, or god.

AMAZON A term for a large strong woman that comes from the name for a group of female warriors in Greek mythology.

ANTECHAMBER A room which serves as an entrance to another room.

AYUTHIA Also known as Ayutthaya, this city was the capital of Siam from 1350 to 1767.

BETEL An Asian climbing plant.

BOLSTER A round, narrow pillow which is as long as a bed.

BRAHMAN 1. A priest of the Hindu religion. 2. A member of the highest class of the Hindu religion, often a priest.

BREADFRUIT The fruit of a tree found in the tropics.

BUDDHA The man who founded the faith of Buddhism, which is based upon meditation and simple living. Buddhism was founded in eastern Asia in the sixth century B.C

CHOLERA An infectious disease which usually causes serious intestinal disorders and has caused many deadly outbreaks.

CIRCULAR A statement or notice printed for distribution to a certain group.

CONSULATE The office of a consul, a person who resides in a foreign country in order to protect his or her native country's citizens or commercial interests.

DAGUERREOTYPE An early photograph made by using light sensitive metallic plates.

DIRGE A song or hymn of mourning.

DOWAGER A widow whose property or title was inherited from her husband.

EURASIAN A person of European and Asian descent.

FEUDALISM A social, political, and economic system in medieval Europe in which a lord granted land to a member of his estate in return for military or other services.

FEZ A tall hat without a brim, usually tasseled and made of felt.

HAREM The wives and concubines of one man.

HINDUSTANI Of or related to a particular region in India.

ILEX Any tree or shrub in the holly family.

JESSAMINE A climbing plant that usually has fragrant white flowers. Also known as jasmine.

JUNK A tall Chinese boat.

KRAAL A fenced pen, usually for cattle or sheep.

MALAY The language spoken on the Malay peninsula, on which the official language of Indonesia is based.

MANDARIN A member of one of the nine classes of officials in the Chinese Empire.

MOHAMMEDAN A believer in the religion of Islam.

MULLAH A leader or teacher of the religion of Islam.

MUSLIN A plain fabric of woven cotton.

OLEANDER A shrub with clusters of red or white blossoms.

PERSIA A country in the Middle East now known as Iran.

PALI The sacred language of early Buddhist writings.

PANUNG A Siamese garment often worn as a loincloth.

POMELO A type of grapefruit.

QUAY A wharf or man-made landing space used by boats for loading purposes.

REGENT One who rules in the name and place of another ruler.

RETINUE The group of attendants of a person of rank.

ROOD A piece of land which measures one fourth of an acre.

SALA A reception room or hall which acts as a meeting place.

SALAAM An Oriental greeting or gesture of respect or reverence made by placing the palm of the right hand on the forehead and bowing low.

SALON A drawing room in which guests are received.

SANSKRIT An ancient language of the Hindus of India.

TONSURE The shaving of the head of a priest or a monk.